The Homecoming *includes bonus short story* When They Were Young

Editor: Talia Leduc

ISBN-13: 978-1998775668

Give feedback on the book at:
lorhainneeckhart@hotmail.com

Twitter: @LEckhart
Facebook: AuthorLorhainneEckhart

Printed in the U.S.A

The Homecoming

THE FRIESSENS
BOOK TWENTY-FOUR

LORHAINNE ECKHART

The Friessen Family Series
Reading order:

The Outsider Series

The Forgotten Child
A Baby And A Wedding
Fallen Hero
The Awakening
Secrets
Runaway
Overdue
The Unexpected Storm
The Wedding

The Friessens: A New Beginning

The Deadline
The Price to Love
A Different Kind of Love
A Vow of Love, A Friessen Family Christmas

The Friessens

The Reunion
The Bloodline
The Promise
The Business Plan
The Decision
First Love
Family First
Leave the Light On
In the Moment
In the Family: A Friessen Family Christmas
In the Silence
In the Stars
In the Charm
Unexpected Consequences
It Was Always You
The First Time I Saw You
Welcome to My Arms
Welcome to Boston (A Paige & Morgan Short Story)
I'll Always Love You
Ground Rules
A Reason to Breathe
You Are My Everything
Anything For You
The Homecoming includes When They Were Young
Stay Away From My Daughter
The Bad Boy
A Place of Our Own
The Visitor
All About Devon
Long Past Dawn
How to Heal a Heart
Keep Me In Your Heart

The Friessen Family

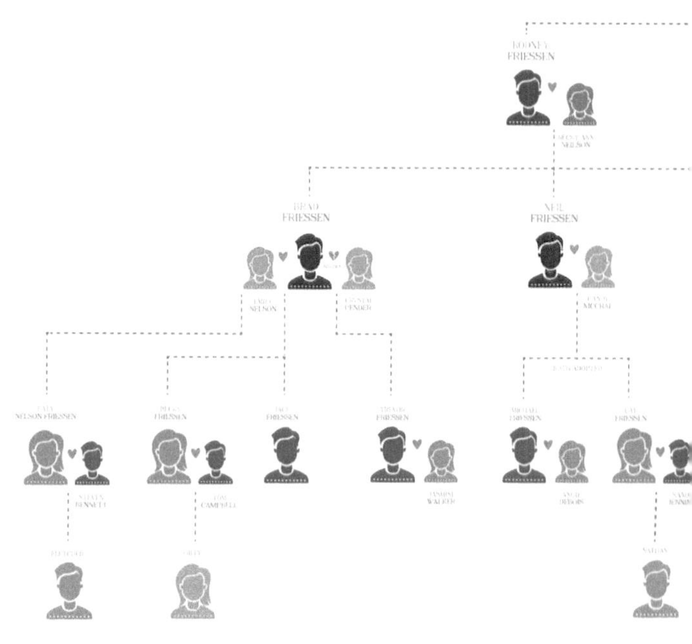

<table>
<tr><td>

The Outsider Series

THE FORGOTTEN CHILD	BRAD & EMILY
A BABY AND A WEDDING	BRAD & EMILY &
FALLEN HERO	JED, DIANA & ANDY
THE SEARCH	JED, DIANA & ANDY
THE AWAKENING	ANDY & LAURA

</td><td>

The Outsider Series

SECRETS	DIANA & JED
RUNAWAY	ANDY & LAURA
OVERDUE	JED & DIANA
THE UNEXPECTED STORM	NEIL & CANDY
THE WEDDING	NEIL & CANDY

</td><td>

The Friessens: A New Beginning

THE DEADLINE	ANDY & LAURA
THE PRICE TO LOVE	NEIL & CANDY
A DIFFERENT KIND OF LOVE	BRAD & EMILY
A VOW OF LOVE	THE ENTIRE
A FRIESSEN FAMILY CHRISTMAS	FRIESSEN FAMILY

</td></tr>
</table>

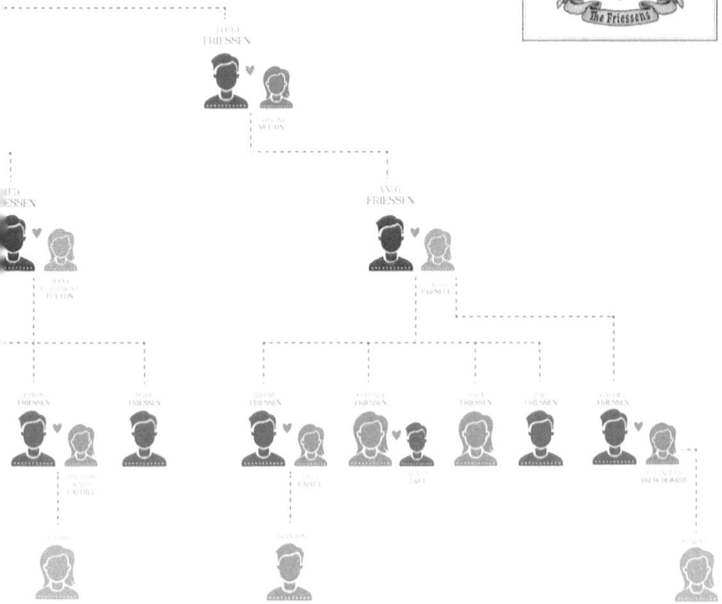

TODD FRIESSEN — CAROLINE MCCAIN

TED FRIESSEN — HANNA ULTON

ANDY FRIESSEN — KATY BARNETT

The Friessens

THE ENTIRE FRIESSEN FAMILY	LEAVE THE LIGHT ON	KATY & STEVEN
ANDY & LAURA	IN THE MOMENT	BECKY & TOM
TED & DIANA	IN THE FAMILY	THE ENTIRE FRIESSEN FAMILY
NEIL & LANG	IN THE SILENCE	CALE & NANCIE
BRAD & FAMILY	IN THE STARS	DANNY & EVIE
KATY & STEVEN	IN THE CHARM	CHRIS & EJ
KATY & STEVEN	UNEXPECTED CONSEQUENCES	CHRIS & EJ

The Friessens

IT WAS ALWAYS YOU	KATY & STEVEN
THE FIRST TIME I SAW YOU	GABRIEL & ELIZABETH
WELCOME TO MY ARMS	CHELSEA & SLADE
WELCOME TO BOSTON	PAIGE & MORGAN
I'LL ALWAYS LOVE YOU	JEREMY
GROUND RULES	JEREMY & LILY
A REASON TO BREATHE	TREVOR & JASMINE
YOU ARE MY EVERYTHING	MICHAEL & ANGIE
ANYTHING FOR YOU	
THE HOMECOMING	THE ENTIRE FRIESSEN FAMILY

The Homecoming

A FAMILY REUNION WITH AN EDGE OF YOUR SEAT TWIST.

A seemingly perfect reunion until one fateful moment three lives are put in danger, the fallout could ultimately shatter the deep love and trust in this family, dividing them forever—and the cost could be something far greater than any of them could have imagined.

"Several of our favorite characters are put in danger and a serious secret is revealed by someone you'd never suspect."

(PATTI B.)

"A Friessen book would not be complete without family drama and boy does this one deliver the drama, almost from page one!"

–H. MITCHELL

Catch up with your favorite family, the Friessens, as four generations come together for what they anticipate to be a fun-filled weekend with babies and children, loads of love, and laughter. You can expect all the drama of young love, from the secrets to the hidden truths in a seemingly perfect marriage.

However, one fateful moment changes everything in this unforgettable story. When three lives are put in danger, the fallout could ultimately shatter the deep love and trust in this family, dividing them forever—and the cost could be something far greater than any of them could have imagined.

CHAPTER

One

"So what was that about?" Emily asked, appearing tired. They had just travelled six hours on a cramped overbooked flight from Seattle that had been delayed by nearly ninety minutes. She yawned and swept her fingers through her shoulder-length brown hair, which was slowly becoming lighter from the highlights she kept adding to hide the spots of gray.

Brad glanced at his Android before tucking it in the back pocket of his jeans and taking in the conveyor belt at the Cancun airport. On it were a single black suitcase and two boxes tied together. Not one of the bags from their flight had been unloaded, and they had been standing there for nearly ten minutes. He was still puzzled by the message his dad had left.

"I don't know," he said. "Weird, is all—something about whether I could call him back to confirm who all is coming to stay with them…"

Did Rodney mean for the next weekend? He'd give it another listen, as it made no sense. The entire family was travelling there, all the kids and grandkids, to stay at the

Cancun resort together for the first time. They had even booked rooms in the same wing. Jed and Diana and their brood were also on the way, as were Andy and Laura and theirs. His mom and dad knew that was the plan.

He was starting to wonder if his dad was becoming more forgetful. It wasn't like him to leave that kind of scatterbrained message. He rolled his shoulders, feeling restless after having to sit for so long and feeling the angst of his family around him, their ups and downs, the bickering of Becky and Tom.

"Maybe we should swing over to the house first before we check in, make sure everything's good," Brad said.

Emily's jaw slackened, and he wasn't sure what she was about to say.

"Have you seen Neil?" Candy said, appearing beside him, her long dark hair freshly cut to shoulder length.

He spotted Xander and Cat also walking their way. Xander had a deep brooding look and a perpetual five o'clock shadow, his jeans riding low with a swagger. He held Cat's hand, and she appeared lost in thought. Brad was still stuck on the sight of her new hair, red with dark lowlights.

"No, I haven't, not since we got off the plane," he said. "Trevor!" he called out and waved, seeing his son was holding Jasmine's hand, pressed against a concrete wall.

Trevor began pulling her along over to them, and what was she doing but holding her hand over her eyes, following him blindly? Of course, a number of odd looks were passed their way. The Cancun airport was crowded and chaotic, and he'd forgotten how loud and noisy it was, concrete and old.

Something seemed to be up, a strangeness, an energy he couldn't put his finger on—or maybe it had just been too long since he'd been there. They were all feeling the heightened sense of worry, stress, or expectation, and likely the restlessness of having travelled all day, too, not to mention the fact that they were all still dressed for the Seattle rain. Maybe some time to decompress by the pool with a beer, catching up with his family, would definitely help. Yeah, he couldn't wait.

"Mom, can you take Gilly?" Becky said. "Tom's on the phone again, and I have to go to the bathroom." She was wearing a ratty old oversized T-shirt and dark-rimmed glasses, with deep circles under her eyes, and her hair was pulled up in a really messy bun. He'd never expected to see this kind of harried expression on her face. His granddaughter, Gilly, was crying and kicking to get down, her nose running and her blue eyes filled with tears. She was fast coming up on the terrible twos.

"Here, come to Gramps," he said and reached for her, immediately feeling her soaked-through diaper under her floral dress, which was riding up. She was barefoot like she always was. "She's wet, Becky—and where is Tom?"

Emily patted Gilly's back, and she whimpered, staring up at him and tossing her head back. Becky wasn't the greatest at changing the baby's diapers, and Gilly, he swore, had the mischief of all his kids combined in one. Becky just lifted her hand and let out a frustrated sigh. He could see her patience was wearing thin.

"Over there, on the phone. Some hospital emergency, he said. Don't know why he's insisted on calling back. Family holiday means just that, a holiday, with no work, not sticking me with everything." Becky actually slipped the diaper bag off her shoulder, and for a second he thought she'd dump it on the ground, but Emily grabbed it. He took in Cat, who was now talking to Candy. Both also seemed on edge as they looked around.

"Dad, where're our suitcases?" Trevor asked. Jasmine was making a weird noise with her mouth.

"Be patient," Brad said. "They'll be here soon."

Becky was already walking toward the bathroom when Fletcher, Jack, Katy, and Steven appeared. He could smell an odor and knew it was Gilly.

"Okay, you can't wait. You need changed now," Brad said as he held out his granddaughter, then spotted the luggage after hearing the thump of the first suitcase dumping down the conveyor belt. "You need to talk to your daughter about taking better care of Gilly," he said.

Emily frowned and shook her head. "Hey, just as easy for you to have a talk with her, as well. Come on, Gilly. Grandma will change your diaper."

Brad passed Gilly over just as Candy tapped his arm.

"I still can't find Neil," she said. He wasn't sure what to make of her expression—off, anxious. Over what, he didn't know.

"Well, I'm sure he couldn't have gone far…" he started to say just as he spotted his brother walking toward them with Cat and Xander's baby boy tucked into a baby carrier strapped across his chest. He looked ridiculous and happy in Bermuda shorts and sandals, working a piece of gum. This casual, laid-back Neil was a lot to get used to.

"Dad, where were you?" Cat said. "You can't keep taking off with the baby…" She reached for baby Nathan, who was the spitting image of Xander, with big eyes, thick dark lashes, and the same intense expression. He was unbelievably quiet, easy, the exact opposite of Gilly.

"No one thought to grab the bags?" Neil said. "Thought we'd be out of here." He was still wearing the carrier and had a diaper bag over his shoulder. "And you can thank me, Cat. I changed the baby. He's hungry, too."

Over by the conveyer, Katy was saying something to

Trevor, and Steven was pulling a luggage cart over and grabbing luggage off. While it was great having a son-in-law to take care of things for him, Brad figured he should help.

"So I had a message from Dad," he said. "I think I'll swing by the house first before the resort. He seemed under the impression we're all coming next week and that we're staying there?"

Neil gave him the oddest look and then just shook his head. "Seriously?" he said. "Well, if you are, bring them back with you to the resort. I'm sure Diana, Jed, and their crew are already there. Andy, too, I think. I got a text from him that they arrived earlier today. I would've thought Jed or Andy would call them." Neil pulled his iPhone from his pocket and scanned his messages.

Brad then spotted Xander, who had a second luggage cart, over by Steven. The two of them were handling, talking, giving Jack and Fletcher orders, and tossing bags onto the luggage carts. He gestured with his chin. "You think they got everything?"

Neil laughed softly. "Hope so. One of the benefits, I'd think, of having to put up with a son-in-law. Let them get it."

Emily and Becky were walking back side by side, Emily holding Gilly on her hip. His daughter appeared far from put together, but at least Tom was off his call and was now over by Steven, tossing a bag on one of the carts.

"Dad, Jasmine needs to go," Trevor called out. Jasmine was now standing close to him, staring at the ground and moving side to side. She was over-stimulated, over-everything.

"Katy, take Trevor and Jasmine and start heading through customs," he said, but just then, Steven headed over, pushing one of the luggage carts, and he gestured with his thumb to Brad and said, "We got all the bags. Let's go."

Neil's phone dinged, and his expression changed as he stared at the screen.

"What is it?" Brad asked.

Neil shook his head. Everyone was talking and following Steven, Xander, and the carts to the final check point. "Not sure… A text from Andy. He asked if we've heard from Mom and Dad."

Candy was pulling on his arm, saying something, and he just shook his head. Emily, Becky, and Tom were now standing there, staring at them as if they'd just figured out something was up.

"You know what?" Neil said. "Maybe I'll join you and stop in at Mom and Dad's."

"What, why? What's going on?" Becky piped in. Tom scooped Gilly into his arms and kissed her cheek.

"Nothing, most likely, but…you talk to your grandma?" Brad said. He knew Becky talked more with his mom than anyone else in the family.

Becky pushed the bridge of her glasses up her nose and shrugged. "Not since yesterday. Why, what's up?" She was looking from him to Neil, and so were Emily and Candy, too.

"Just a message from your grandpa. Seems like he thinks we're not coming until next week and that we're staying there. So I think Neil and I will swing by there first. You all go on to the resort and get checked in."

Becky never blinked and then slowly turned to Neil. "That's ridiculous," she said. "They know we're coming today. Grandma and I are booked in for a pedicure after dinner tonight at the resort. If you're going to drop in on Gram and Gramps, then I'm coming, too."

Tom just shook his head and walked away.

"You should go to the hotel with your husband, Becky, and your daughter," Brad said, but what did his daughter do but shake her head? She was pure stubbornness.

"No, I'm going with you," she said. "Besides, I want a minute aside to talk to Grams without everyone there and without Tom passing Gilly off to me."

Then Becky was walking off, and Emily levelled a hard look his way, which he knew well meant he needed to do something about their daughter. That left four: Candy, Neil, Emily, and him.

"Do you think if we hang back here for a second, they'll forget we're here?" Neil said just as Candy tapped his chest.

"Oh, stop it," she said. "Why don't we let the rest of them head on to the resort, and the four of us can stop in and see your parents?" She lifted her chin to where the Mexican security agents were looking through the largest black suitcase. "And Becky," she added as an afterthought, likely because she knew well how stubborn his daughter was.

Brad looked over to where Katy and Steven were herding Jack, Fletcher, Trevor, and Jasmine through the checkpoint. Then there were Tom and Becky and Gilly, Cat and Xander and Nathan, and as they all passed through, he couldn't see them anymore.

This was meant to be a fun-filled reunion, but it seemed something else was brewing in the wind that he couldn't put his finger on.

CHAPTER

Two

"Neil, who are you texting now?" Candy said.

He could see the three dots that meant Xander was considering how to answer his last text: a long thinking pause, then no response. "Just making sure Cat has everything she needs for Nathan. I asked the manager to make sure there's a crib, fresh cotton blankets, nothing synthetic, plenty of drinking water…"

He glanced up, taking in the shock on Emily and Candy's faces. Brad raised his brows—mocking him, he was sure. Becky didn't seem too interested from where she sat beside Candy in the limo, looking out the window, lost in thought. He was still staring at a blank screen, about to send a second text to Xander, when Candy took his phone from his hands and powered it off.

"You're being ridiculous and overstepping again," she said. "Leave them alone. Seriously, Neil, this over-the-top obsessive need of yours has got to stop. Xander can look after them. The baby is fine."

Brad said nothing but appeared close to laughing at

him, and he watched as his wife tucked his phone in her purse.

"Hey, he's my grandson," Neil said. "I just want to make sure he has everything he needs…" And he wanted to make sure Cat was comfortable, too, because the dogs weren't there to help her. He just couldn't shake the need to be close to his grandson and worry about anything and everything that could go wrong.

This time, Brad was laughing and shaking his head. "Just admit it, Neil. You won't be happy until you have everyone living under your roof. Just get a bigger house so you can stick your nose into their business all the time. Oh, wait! You're over at Cat's almost every day now, and you even have Nathan stay over at your place how often…?"

"Well, at least Uncle Neil cares," Becky spoke up.

The shock and surprise on everyone's face mirrored his, he thought, as they took the turnoff to his parents' estate, up the long driveway lined by trees that had grown back. He'd never heard her speak that way, and he took in Emily's expression as she lifted her hand, at a loss.

"Becky, are you kidding me? What's going on with you?" she said.

"Nothing, sorry. Shouldn't have said anything." Becky lifted her hand to wave it off, and he could feel how on edge she was. Even Candy tossed him an uneasy look. Brad was levelling that shrewd gaze on her, the tough-love one he'd seen a time or two when the kids were growing up.

"What is this about, Becky? You don't get to play that game, saying we don't care and then never mind. You're a grown woman, a mother…" Brad didn't pull his gaze away, but Becky was stubborn—just like Brad in so many ways. Neil wondered who'd blink first.

"Are you needing a break with the baby? Is that what

this is?" Emily finally broke the standoff. He wanted to reach out and tell her to stop, especially the way she was looking imploringly at Becky, always trying to make it easier.

"Well, I kind of have one now because I didn't give Tom a choice, right?" she said.

Even to Neil, that didn't sound like Becky. He found himself leaning forward to see the stubborn set of her jaw, the way she glanced from Brad to Emily and then back to the estate.

They pulled up and parked, but he thought Brad might still have another thing or two to say. Instead, Becky had the door open and was stepping out. Brad just shook his head, and Neil raised a brow, wondering what that was all about. He'd missed something big going on between Becky and Tom. Trouble? Maybe.

"Care to share what the issue is?" Neil asked as the four of them remained in the back. The driver was now out of the vehicle, and Becky was heading across the circular driveway, nearly to the front door.

Brad just shook his head, "Mood swings?" he said. "I don't know, but she's really pushing with Tom, and you know I'm not a fan of his."

Emily made a rude noise he'd never heard before and stepped out, and Candy followed.

"So is it work, or not working?" Neil said. "Is there trouble, she wants to leave him…what?"

Brad just shook his head and climbed out. Neil took his time, taking in his brother as he handed a cash tip to the driver. Candy and Emily were already walking to the house.

"It's locked," Becky called out, then rapped the brass knocker on the front door and pressed the bell. He could hear the chime from outside.

"Maybe Mom and Dad are at the resort?" Neil said. "But Maria and Carlos should still be here."

"They don't work here anymore," Becky said.

Candy tried to open the door, but it was locked, and she tossed Neil an uneasy gaze. Brad was over at the huge window to the sunken living room.

"Drapes are pulled. Can't see in," he said, then tapped on the window, but they didn't hear anything.

"Since when are Maria and Carlos not here?" Neil said. The look Candy gave him showed it was the first she was hearing of it, too.

Becky just shrugged. He took in how not put together she was, in her faded oversized shirt and baggy ultra-worn jeans, wearing flip flops. The glasses were new, too. He wondered if she'd bothered to brush her hair before pulling it up in a messy bun.

The limo was already pulling away when Brad shoved his fingers in his mouth and whistled. The driver should have stopped, but he kept going down the driveway and was gone around the bend, the trees blocking them from view.

"Let's walk around back. Maybe they're out at the pool," Brad said.

"Or not here," Candy suggested. "Neil, don't you have a key still?"

Neil walked around the house, taking in the empty driveway that led to the garage in back. He jammed his hands in his pockets, but his keys weren't there. They were tucked in his bags, on their way to the resort. "Not with me," he tossed out over his shoulder.

Brad was close behind him, his cowboy boots scraping against the walkway. He wore blue jeans and a deep blue T-shirt, but at least it was short sleeved. His hair was now a mix of dark and white. He squinted in the bright sun and pulled his phone from his pocket, then texted something and shook his head. "Jed and Andy are at the pool," he said. "Haven't seen Mom and Dad."

They took in the back of the house. The pool still had the vinyl cover over it, and the patio furniture was in the same place he remembered. The umbrella was down as if his mom and dad hadn't been out that day.

"Mom, Dad!" Brad cupped his hands and called out. He was loud, and Neil expected to hear something. He reached for the back door that led into the kitchen to find that it was locked, and Brad walked over to the double doors off the dining room and tried the knob, both of them. Locked. He just shook his head.

"Well, this is really strange," Neil said, taking in Candy, Emily, and Becky, who had her arms crossed over her breasts. She was far from the happy girl he'd known. When had she slipped into this?

"Well, maybe you should call the resort, get a car out here for us," Brad said.

Neil held his hand out to Candy. "Can I have my phone?"

Just then, there was the click of a lock, and the door opened. Neil took in the dark eyes and dark hair of the man who had answered—in his early fifties, maybe. "Can I help you?" he said in a deep voice, a southern accent that was more a twang than a drawl.

Neil laughed, only it wasn't a laugh, because this was ridiculous. "Yeah, who are you?" he said. "Where are my parents, Rodney and Becky Friessen?"

The man was tall, broad shouldered, in a ratty T-shirt and jeans, with a scar at his jawline. "I work here, manage the estate. Who are you?" The man looked at him and then dragged his gaze over to Brad, and it wasn't lost on him that he was standing in the doorway, blocking it as if they were unwelcome guests.

"Are my mom and dad here, Becky and Rodney?" Brad said.

The man took in Brad as if he suspected he would cause trouble, then pulled his gaze back to Neil, who expected him to step back and let them in, but he didn't. The unease he'd been feeling earlier now felt more like a vise, squeezing all the air out of his chest.

"Nope," the man said and made a face, and Neil thought he was going to close the door on them.

"Look," he said. "We're family. I'm Neil, and that's my brother Brad. Our wives are over there, and my niece. Surely my parents said to expect us?" He wondered if maybe Jed was behind this—a joke, maybe. He found himself trying to see past the man when he felt a hand slam into his chest to stop him.

"All I can say is they're not here," the man said, "and they said nothing about family coming. If you don't mind, I'd rather not take chances. This is private property. You're trespassing, and I'm tasked with looking after this property and all. There have been break-ins, a lot over the last while, men breaking in and living in empty homes, taking them over, so if it's all the same to you…" He didn't smile. He had a kind of hardness that let Neil know they weren't getting past him.

The phone was ringing inside, and Neil glanced over to see Brad with his cell phone to his ear. The man only glanced once over his shoulder, and he was tempted to push past. This was crazy, ridiculous.

"Well, see here," Brad said. "We're not leaving, and you haven't answered us about our parents. Where are they? That's me calling." He held his cell phone up and then ended the call as if proving a point, as the ringing stopped inside. "What is your name?"

Neil wondered when it was that Maria and Carlos had left and where his parents had found someone like this.

"Davis," the man replied. "Now, as I said…"

"Davis, great," Brad interrupted. "There seems to have been a miscommunication somewhere. I appreciate this vigilance and you taking your job seriously, protecting this estate, but I'm sure if you get my mom and dad on the phone, they'll tell you…" A phone was ringing inside again, quieter this time, and Brad was holding up his cell. "That would be me calling my dad's cell phone. So, again, where are my parents?"

It happened so fast.

Davis reached behind his back, and there was a gun. He flicked the safety and pointed it straight out to the women.

Neil stepped back, his hands up, hearing a gasp and shriek—Candy or maybe Emily. It was so precise, Davis's stance, his familiarity with the gun. Neil could always tell when someone lived and breathed guns, knew how to hold and use them. The man appeared to be one with the weapon.

"Whoa, whoa! What is this? Let's just keep it together, here," Neil said.

Davis held the gun, aiming as if he knew what he was doing. He didn't even glance his way as he jabbed his right hand to Neil. "Take a step back, both of you, because right now I have the babe in the glasses in my sights, and I never miss. So back the fuck up. There's no second chance. I ask you to do something once, and the next time I pull the trigger."

"Okay, just relax," Brad said. "Here, put the gun on me, not my daughter."

Neil couldn't pull his eyes away from the threat to his family. He was the one standing between them, and Brad took a step away from the house, over to the women. He couldn't believe this was happening. Where were his mom and dad?

He dared to glance only once behind him to Candy, Emily, and Becky knowing the shock on their faces did little to help this situation. Like, what the hell was going on here? His mom and dad, were they inside? Were they hurt? They weren't answering. Candy, Emily, Becky, and Brad… they were all in deep shit.

He went to reach out to Candy when he heard the distinct sound of a gun being cocked, a sound that chilled him to the bone.

"You two don't listen, do you?" Davis said. Then the gun fired with a pop.

He heard a scream, long and loud, and Brad roared.

Davis flicked the gun over to him. "Why is it that everyone has to make everything so damn hard? I told you I'd only say it once. If you just listened and did as you were told, I wouldn't have shot her."

Three

"Andy, you hear back from Neil or Brad yet?" Jed said from where he lay on the lounger in orange striped trunks, still wet from the pool, wearing a straw hat and shades under the bright Mexico sun. A waitress took his empty beer bottle from the table beside him and rested two more ice-cold Coronas with limes in its place. He was finally feeling as if he was decompressing.

Andy was in the other lounger next to him, the plastic side table between them. He picked up one of the beers and squeezed the lime in as he shook his head, then lifted it and took a swallow. "Nope, not since Brad texted to say they were at the house. Odd, is all I can say. Hope they hurry up. I thought Rodney and Becky would be at the resort to meet us. They knew we were coming in earlier."

Diana and Laura were in the pool, Laura in a green and white two-piece bathing suit, Diana in a light blue tankini. Danny, Chris, Mark, Jeremy, and Zac were in the pool, too, playing volleyball and making enough noise that it was hard to miss the competition between them. He was pretty sure JD and Evie were in their adjoining rooms with Ally and Sophie, who were down for a nap.

"Grandpa, I'm hungry!" called Brandon. "And Mom said no to cheesy nachos." He wore blue swim trunks and was barefoot.

Jed still couldn't believe Jeremy was now married and had fathered a kid so young.

Andy lifted Brandon and sat him on his lap in the lounger. "Well, you stay here with me. If your mom said no to nachos, you know that's the answer. Where is Tiffy, anyway?"

Jed dragged his gaze across the courtyard to the other lounge chairs that surrounded the infinity pool, a waterfall bridge to the right and one of the outdoor restaurants behind them. He could smell the food, which he knew from memory was spicy and exceptional.

"She's over there," Brandon said and pointed, and Jed had to hide a smile at the little boy's disappointment. Maybe he had expected Andy to override his mom. Brandon was a charmer and smart as all hell, and he figured out quickly whom he could work and whom he couldn't. Jed couldn't help following the direction he pointed, seeing Tiffy walking their way with Elizabeth and Shaunty, everyone in swimsuits and carrying towels. She must have noticed Brandon was with Andy, as she lifted her hand and waved, and they took up three lounge chairs about six chairs down.

"Hey, Dad," Chelsea said as she appeared behind Andy, her long dark hair wavy, wearing a purple sundress, all smiles. Alaric, her husband, was behind her, dark, tall, and rugged, wearing khaki shorts and a white T-shirt. He just had a look, Jed swore, that said he was connected to the Italian mafia.

"When did you get here?" Andy said. Man, did he love his kids, his family. He jumped up, holding Brandon, then put him on the ground as he pulled Chelsea into a big hug and kissed her cheek before shaking Alaric's hand.

Laura spotted her daughter and squealed as she struggled to climb out of the pool, and Diana put her hand on Laura's butt to push her out. It was hilarious.

"Just got here," Chelsea said. "Checked into our room, dumped our bags, and wanted to find you first."

"Oh, it's so good to see you," Laura said as she hugged Chelsea.

"Mom, you're getting me all wet!" Chelsea was laughing.

Jed took a minute to just see them, all grown up, even though it seemed they'd been born just yesterday. Time was speeding up, even though he felt no different than when he'd been young and first married.

"Get your swimsuit on and join us," Laura said." It's about time you got here. We're all in the pool or sitting by it, like your father, drinking beer." She laughed, and Andy slid his arms teasingly around her even though she was still dripping from the pool.

Gabriel appeared and dumped a towel on the lounger on Andy's other side. "Hey, sis. About time you got here," he said and hugged Chelsea.

Jed lifted his hand to her and Alaric, who strode over to him, maybe to get out of the family hug fest.

He held out his hand over the back of the lounger. "Great to see you again, Jed."

He shook his hand. "You too, Ric."

"You seen Sara?" Andy asked.

Jed just shook his head before spotting her on the other side of the pool with what looked like some teens—boys, of course, who had moved in on the hot blonde. "In the pool, over there," he said and pointed, then watched as Andy dragged his gaze over to where she was floating on a noodle. One light-haired boy was helping her float, no doubt looking to put his hands anywhere on her.

Yup, Andy zeroed in, and it took him only half a second to shove his fingers in his mouth and let out a sharp whistle. "Sara!" he yelled as if she were at the other end of the block. Everyone looked, and likely anyone in Cancun named Sara, too. He gestured for her to come over.

Jed just lifted his beer, took a swallow, and did his best not to laugh over his cousin's predicament.

"Trying to keep her on a short tether, is he?" Alaric said.

Jed looked back at him, wondering what to say, considering he knew well that Andy wasn't handling the teenage daughter thing with much grace. Right now, he was glad they'd had only boys—but then there were his granddaughters. Maybe he wouldn't escape the same fate.

"What is it, Dad?" Sara said as she swam over on the noodle. The boy at the other end climbed out of the pool and disappeared.

"Your sister's here. Why don't you take Brandon and go share a snack?" Andy said.

Sara climbed out of the pool in her skimpy red bikini, showing off her great body, and Andy handed her a towel. Evidently, she understood, and she took the towel in one hand and held her other out to Brandon. After she said something to Chelsea, the three of them were gone, Alaric with them.

"Jed, there're the kids," Andy said, letting his hand linger on his wife's ass for a second, her arm around his waist. "Xander, Cat! Steven, Katy!" he called out and lifted his hand.

Jed took in Brad's crew as the two little boys, Fletcher

and Jack, jumped into the pool, splashing everyone. "Is your dad here yet?" he said to Katy, who was still dressed in blue jeans and a sleeveless blouse.

"No, not yet. They were at Gramma and Grampa's. They're supposed to be coming back with them. Becky is there, too. Tom was asking if they're on their way back. I guess she's not answering. Thought we'd head out here and find you, see if you know anything about what's going on." Katy leaned over the back of his chair and lifted his straw hat to rest it on her own head.

"No, all is quiet, apparently," Jed said. "Was just asking Andy if he'd heard back from them, and he said no. Hopefully they're on their way here. Great to see you, by the way. You look good." He couldn't remember the last time he'd seen Katy, not since she and Steven had found their way back to each other.

Katy reached down and patted his shoulder. "You, too."

He heard a crying child and looked, seeing Tom striding their way, holding a blond toddler in his arms. That had to be Gilly, wearing a sundress, barefoot, fussing.

"Hey, Katy," Tom said. "I can't get a hold of Becky. She's not answering her phone, and Gilly wants her mother. You hear back from Brad or Neil? Anybody?" Tom was rubbing Gilly's back, and she had her finger in her mouth. Tears were running down her face. Unhappy, overtired, and it looked like she was getting to her dad. Jed remembered those days. He winced as he took another swallow of his beer.

"No, I haven't. Here, do you want me to take Gilly? Come to your auntie," Katy said and held her arms out. Gilly, though, said a stubborn no and put her head into her dad's shoulder. Tom looked as if he was getting close to the end of his rope, as Gilly was still whining and crying—an overtired toddler.

"I just tried texting both Brad and Neil, and they're not answering," Andy said. Laura was sitting at the edge of the pool again, this time holding Cat and Xander's baby.

Steven appeared behind him and lifted his hand in a hello before resting it around Katy. "I just tried calling Brad, Emily, Candy, and Neil on their cell phones," he said. "No one is answering."

Xander was holding Cat's hand, his dark hair wavy, and he had his cell phone to his ear, looking around. Mysterious. Jed still hadn't figured him out. Xander just shook his head. "Not like them to not answer. Especially Neil. He was texting me nonstop, and now silence…"

Jed had to stifle a smile as he lifted the bottle to his mouth and took a swallow, knowing how much Xander and Neil butted heads, most likely because of Neil's incessant need to micromanage just about everyone and every situation.

"Anyone hear from Rodney and Becky? No one is answering the house phone," Xander continued, his phone to his ear.

Tom didn't look impressed. Seemed as if there was stress or trouble between Tom and Becky, or maybe Jed was reading too much into it. "You know, I have half a mind to just go over there and find out what's going on," Tom said.

Xander just pulled his phone away and pressed end, glancing down to Cat, who had said nothing. "No answer at the house. Maybe they're already on their way back. So why don't we get changed and come back for a swim?"

Jed knew Andy well, and the glance he exchanged with him didn't set him at ease. "So no one is answering their phones or texts, and Mom and Dad still aren't answering?"

he said and sat forward. "You know, one or two, no big deal, but everyone?"

Tom managed to pass Gilly over to Katy. "I'm going to grab a cab and head over," he said.

"Just wait." Xander put his hand on Tom's shoulder. "They could already be on their way back. Let's just give them a little longer. We're all tired from travelling, and they're likely just getting caught up and lost track of time. I'm sure they'll be here anytime, Neil leading the way to make sure I haven't screwed something up with his grandson."

Jed nearly choked at Xander's comment, but at least it brought the hint of a smile to Tom.

"Yeah, Xander's right," Andy started. "They're probably visiting, talking, and…"

"And not hearing their phones?" Jed said. From the look Andy gave him, he knew he was saying it on behalf of everyone.

"That's a lot of phones no one's hearing," said Steven. "One, yeah, okay. Two, sure—but everyone?"

Something about Steven breaking it all down added to the knot that was tightening in Jed's gut. He'd felt off for a while and had been hoping a beer or two would settle him.

"I'm going over there," Tom said and lifted his hands, out of patience.

"Hang on a second. I'll come with you," Xander said, all the teasing gone.

"Yup, I'll tag along too," Steven said, and the three were already walking the other way.

"Wait," Jed called out. He put his bare feet on the hot concrete of the poolside patio and glanced over to Andy before standing up, resting his beer on the table, and reaching for his key card. "I'll go with you. Just give me a minute to get some pants on, and maybe by the time I'm dressed, they'll already be here."

Even as he said it, though, he knew deep down that what he was hoping for was a tall tale they could all laugh over, like everyone's phone batteries had died all at the same time.

"Right," he said under his breath.

There was so much blood, and her eyes were wide with shock and fear—and who the hell was screaming? No, not screaming. Becky was hyperventilating, panting as Emily held her, blood splattered on her face, her hands in the air, shaking.

The sticky ooze of blood covered Brad's hands as he pressed them over her thigh, over the bullet wound. Davis had shot his daughter, and he could feel the man standing behind him. He knew the gun was still pointed his way and could vaguely hear Neil yelling, saying something to him, but the words, none of them made sense.

He felt for the first time in his life as if someone was taking someone he loved from him. It was horrible, the feeling of surrealness. He'd never felt so damn helpless in his life.

"Brad, your belt! Take it off and wrap it above the bullet. Pull tight to stop the bleeding," Candy snapped and pressed her hands over the wound when he moved his aside. She put pressure on the bleeding, and Becky screamed as he fumbled for his belt, seeing the tears streaming down Emily's face as Becky leaned against her. Emily's arms were around her chest, holding her against her, trying to keep her calm. She was kissing her cheek, mumbling, "It's going to be okay. Just breathe. I got you, I got you, I love you…"

Brad pulled at his belt, but it stuck on one of the loops, and he yanked and yanked before pulling it free and slipping it under Becky's leg. She cried out. Her glasses were crooked, and she knocked them away from her face.

"Higher, Brad," Candy said. "Right there, yes. Pull it through and tighten it." She turned to the man and shouted over her shoulder, "We need to get her to the hospital! She's going to bleed to death."

Brad pulled the belt tight. Becky was groaning, and he could see how much he was hurting her. Her hands were shaking, and she was so damn pale. "You just stay with me, you hear me? You keep your eyes open and on me. I'm going to get you to a hospital. I'm going to get you help."

He stood up, seeing the life in his daughter's eyes draining out of her. She was on the brink of living or dying, and nothing was going to keep him from doing everything to get her out of there and save her life. He didn't care that Davis was holding a gun. He'd take a bullet first.

"You son of a bitch! I'll kill you with my bare hands! We're leaving. I'm taking my daughter to the hospital."

The gun, which had been levelled on Neil, swung over to him along with the unfeeling eyes of the man holding it. Davis angled his head and shook it, so controlled. "No, you're not. Sit on down on the ground, or the next bullet won't be a flesh wound in the leg. I'll put it right between her eyes."

In the second in which he pulled in a breath, he could hear the thumping of his heart, long loud, and nothing else. He believed Davis would simply do exactly what he said he would. He took in his daughter's blood on his hands, and he went down on his knees, seeing the man nod.

"Good to see you learn fast."

"My daughter needs a hospital. I'll stay. Let her go," Brad said.

Davis was shaking his head, and he glanced over to Becky. "I've seen worse. She'll live." He stepped back. "Bring her inside the house, you and you." He pointed with his gun to Brad and Neil and then stepped outside, pointing it back at Becky.

It took Brad a second to pull it together. Neil was down beside Candy, his hand on hers, and Brad couldn't pull his eyes from Emily. She was imploring him to do something. He slid his hand under Becky, around her back, under her knees.

"I'm going to lift you up, baby…" he said—and then what? Neil had his hand on Becky's other shoulder and under her, and they lifted.

"What is it you want?" Neil said.

Davis just shook his head. "I said move her inside now. You come over here." He gestured to Candy, who was now standing with Emily.

"Not my wife. You keep your hands off my wife," Neil snapped as they stood up, Becky between them, her arm now over Brad's shoulders. He had one arm behind her back, the other holding under her knees, the belt and gunshot leg against him, and she cried out.

He didn't need Neil to help, and Neil must have known, as he stepped away and reached out to grab Candy, but Davis took one step, grabbed hold of her arm, and yanked her toward him so roughly that she stumbled.

Then he had the gun to Candy's temple, his mouth close to her ear.

"Don't move, there, chica. Would hate to mess up that beautiful face."

Brad stared in horror as Candy shut her eyes so tightly a tear slipped out. She was shaking and frozen with fear.

"I hear you," Neil said. "We hear you. Whatever you want, money, anything—you name it, you got it. Just tell me what it is you want. Let my wife go. Let the women go…"

The way Neil pleaded, Brad thought he would come undone. He was saying everything Brad wanted to say as he held Becky, feeling the way she trembled and leaned her head against him. She didn't look good. Whatever Davis wanted, he'd give it to him just to get his daughter, his wife, his family out of there.

Davis stepped to the side, taking Candy with him, the door wide open. "Take her inside the house, all of you, inside to the living room—and try nothing, because I will shoot her. I don't want to shoot her, but I will."

The way he said it, Brad knew without a shadow of a doubt he would do exactly as he said. At the same time, Davis had said nothing about what he wanted from them.

"Emily, go," Brad said and moved behind his wife to the door. "Neil…"

Neil wouldn't look his way, but he nodded. Brad could see that much, knowing it was killing Neil to see his wife with a gun to her head. He didn't pull his gaze from Candy.

Brad followed Emily into the house, carrying Becky. Inside, it was dark from the curtains being drawn, but light came through the skylights.

Becky was whimpering. "Dad…Tom will know what to do."

He kept moving, and Emily passed him along the hall and to living room.

"Oh no! Becky, Rodney…" she cried out.

As Brad stepped into the entrance of the foyer, he looked right and saw the sunken living room. His mom sat tied to a kitchen chair, her mouth gagged. His dad…where was he? Another guy stood in the living room. He had lighter hair, straight, thinning on top but longish, touching his shoulders. He was thin but the same height as Brad, with an overgrown mustache, a narrow face, and tattoos up his arm. He too held a gun.

"Alan, get them tied up," Davis said.

Brad rested Becky on the sofa and spotted Emily beside the fireplace, on the floor. His dad was lying there, blood dripping from his head, his eyes closed. It was horrible seeing his dad like that, and his first thought was that he was dead. The ache in his chest was so painful that for just a second, he didn't think he could breathe.

"What are you doing?" Alan snapped. "Bring them in. You were supposed to get rid of them."

He wasn't as put together or calm as Davis, and Brad just sat at the edge of the sofa beside his daughter, taking in the way Alan kept flicking his gun toward each of them in turn as if he didn't know where to point it. At any second, it could go off. The man was freaking out, unstable, and it had him thinking they wouldn't get out of there alive.

Brad made himself turn to see his mom, her hair a mess, in a brown floral housecoat. She was gagged and freaking out, and her eyes reached out to him, but what could he do right now? Neil was there now by her side.

"Dad…is he dead?" Brad said.

Emily shook her head. "No. He's breathing, but he's unconscious. His head's bleeding. There's a lot of blood."

His mom was trying to talk against the gag. Davis

shoved Candy away, and she stumbled, but Neil grabbed her and pulled her into his arms. He could hear her trying not to cry but failing miserably.

"It's okay," Neil said. "It's okay, baby. You're going to be okay, I promise you." He had his hand over the back of her head and kissed her cheek, the side of her head.

Alan was walking closer to Emily, his gun on her. "He'll be fine," he said. "Get up. You're going to tie these two up." He looked right at Brad. A chair scraped on the floor, one of the dining chairs.

Davis jabbed the gun and pointed it at him. "We'll start with the big guy first. Brad, is it? Sit." He tossed some rope to Emily, who was now standing, looking helpless, but she caught the rope. It was orange—used for climbing, he thought. "Tie him up, and then we're going to have a chance to get to know each other."

"Dad, please…" Becky started and reached out to him, but Davis was giving him that hard look, and Brad knew what would happen if the orders weren't followed.

Davis held up the gun to Emily, aimed and cocked. He didn't have to say one word, as Brad pulled his hand free from his daughter and took a step, then another, to the chair and sat down, knowing Davis wouldn't hesitate to pull the trigger on his wife. He was racking his brain, trying to figure out what to do. Being tied up and helpless was exactly what couldn't happen.

"Look, I told you, just let everyone else go," Brad said. "I'll stay. You can tie me up, do whatever. Just let them go. You still haven't told us what you want—money or something? You have to want something."

"Tie him, hands behind his back," Davis said, pointing the gun again to Emily.

She was shaking as she strode to him, touched his arm, and went on her knees behind him. He could feel the rope as Emily wrapped it around one wrist and then the other, tying them together. He held his hands back behind the chair and didn't pull his eyes from Davis, whose gun was trained on his wife: steady, deliberate. *Fucking psychopath.*

"Tighter," Davis said, "because if you don't and I have to do it, I won't be happy, and when I'm not happy, someone gets hurt." He moved over to where Becky was on the sofa, leaning on the arm now, and it took everything Brad had in him to stay seated in that chair.

Emily pulled the rope hard, and it bit into his wrist. He hissed.

"Brad, I'm sorry." Her voice was shaking.

"Just tie it. I'm fine," he said, though he was far from it.

Neil still held Candy in his arms, Alan holding his gun on them. Two guns, two men. If it were just him and Neil, they had a chance, but not with Emily, Candy, and Becky. As he'd already figured out, this man wouldn't shoot him and Neil first. It would be the women, the ones they loved.

"Legs too," Davis said. "Tie them to the chair legs, and make sure it's tight, because I'll be checking."

Brad watched his wife crawl on her knees in front of him. She allowed her gaze to linger on him as she wrapped the rope around first one ankle and then the other.

"Up. Up now," Davis said, and Emily took a step back. "Pull that other chair in the corner over here. Alan, you tie up Neil here. Once they're tied up, we'll get the women—"

"My daughter is shot," Brad said, seeing how pale Becky was and the pain she was in. "Look, at least let my wife go and get help. Let my daughter get help." There was so much blood. How long could she hang on?

"I told you before: No one is leaving now," Davis said. "You just insisted on showing up, wouldn't take no for an answer. Your daughter's fate is on you."

He was a cold bastard, unfeeling. Brad was never going

to be able to reason with him, but he pulled in a breath and said, "Fine, I get it. If you won't let her go, then at least let us bring someone in to help. Her husband is a doctor. Let me call him. I'll get him to come over, won't tell him anything, but he can help her. Right now, it's one thing to hold us here, breaking and entering, but murder is different."

The man didn't smile. Brad knew Neil was being tied up by the way he was grunting, but he couldn't pull his gaze from Davis, who was watching him. He didn't know what to make of it before a faint smile touched his lips.

"Doctor? Well, well," he said. "So you've all done well for yourselves, all this, all the money, the resort, the family, kids, grandkids…" At the way he said it, the uneasiness that had settled into Brad's stomach earlier that day now made him feel sick. This wasn't sounding like a random break-in.

"Who are you?" he made himself ask, feeling numb.

He could hear his mom crying behind the gag but couldn't pull his gaze from the man who was responsible for the danger his family was in, and he willed some type of sanity to appear in that moment.

"It's been a lot of years, Brad, Neil—just missing little Jed."

For a minute, he was afraid to breathe. He shifted his gaze over to Neil, seeing shock that mirrored his own.

Davis shrugged and tucked his gun in the front pocket of his jeans. "Robbie Davis," he said. "What's it been, forty-plus years? Was just a kid last time we saw each other. What were we, ten, eleven?"

He blinked.

Neil narrowed his gaze. "Yeah, I remember now. You lived with your dad in that old house, east side of our property."

Brad was still trying to remember the boy from when they were growing up.

Davis let his arms hang and smiled at Neil, but it wasn't the smile of a happy reunion. "Yeah, you'd think that, wouldn't you?" he said. "The thing is, it wasn't your property. It was ours—that is, until your dad stole it right out from under us."

Five

J ed was still feeling a little bit of a buzz from the two beers he'd had with Andy. Add in the hot sun, and he hadn't expected to be doing anything more than hopping into the pool for another swim, some fun, and then dinner later with the family, along with more beer and a chance to catch up with his brothers.

Instead, here he was in the back of a minivan cab, with three rows of seating. Xander was in the front seat, a spot he noted he had been quick to claim, Tom was beside Jed in the second row, and Steven was in the third row alone as they drove through Cancun to where his mom and dad's estate was.

The funny thing was the fact that they had to drive all the way around even though the estate was practically next door. They could have walked along the beach and down the long driveway if there had been a gated entry, but the problem was that Neil had made sure when building the resort to cut off public access to his parents' estate from the beach.

"Still no answer," Xander said and glanced back to

him. "I can tell you this is very unlike Neil. I'm not liking this."

Tom hadn't said anything. He leaned forward in his seat, forearms resting on his knees, still in blue jeans. He was on edge. Jed had opted for shorts, khakis, and sandals only after Diana had stepped into the room while he was pulling on his cowboy boots and told him to take them off. Mexico meant the beach, the pool, and shorts—no cowboy boots. He was feeling out of his element.

"Well, I'm sure there's a reasonable explanation. Relax," he said to Tom as he reached out and patted his shoulder. When he glanced over, Steven tossed him a brooding look as if he didn't buy it, so he decided to change the subject and said, "Steven, are you, Fletcher, and Katy still living at the ranch with Brad and Emily?"

They turned down the tree-lined road, and he knew they weren't far from his mom and dad's. He wasn't sure what to make of the expression on Steven's face, a wince or a smile. He was leaning more toward a wince.

Tom said nothing but pulled his hand over his face, scraping day-old whiskers. Xander was saying something to the driver, likely where to turn.

"Unfortunately, it's more for Fletcher," Steven replied. "He doesn't want to leave. He's grown up there, and, well, it's home, as Brad said. Corinne, my ex, you know, ex-fiancée, is still living in the townhouse I bought when we were together. She managed to get her name on the title after I moved out. I screwed up and am paying the price. She won't leave, and…long story, but the ranch is now home. It's over-crowded, but who knows when we'll leave. Katy's happy, Fletcher's happy, so I suppose that makes me happy."

Jed wasn't sure whether to laugh or what, but he'd suspected Steven had a sarcastic side, and this was it. "And,

Tom, how are you and Becky liking Hoquiam? You're still there and didn't head back to London after the baby?"

Tom leaned back against the seat, and he could see how on edge he was. "It's okay, nice working back in the States, at the hospital. I'm the head of trauma now, which has its perks. It's where I started out. Not sure if Becky's happy, though. She was miserable in London after she finished school. Not sure there's anything I can do that's going to make her happy—go, stay…"

Jed didn't miss the way Steven stared long and hard at Tom. Maybe he knew something he didn't, and he picked up an edge of something that wasn't quite right.

"Is Becky working or home with Gilly?" Steven said.

Tom pulled in a breath, and Steven didn't pull his gaze from him. "She's still home with Gilly. That's her choice, no matter what she says. I told her I'd support her decision, whatever it is, if she wants to work or not, but it seems as if that's something I'm meant to figure out, as she won't tell me. You know that fucking guessing game women do? She wants me to read her mind. I'm supposed to know what she's thinking and feeling. Sometimes it's that she doesn't want to be a mother, and then it's that I work too much, I'm never home, she's alone all the time, I'm not spending time with Gilly… Then there's this jealousy that comes out of nowhere." Tom let out a frustrated sigh, and even Xander glanced back with that dark brooding look he had.

"Well," Xander started, "while you're here in Mexico, you have a built-in family of babysitters, so you can have uninterrupted time with Becky, like a honeymoon of sorts —but with her entire extended family here, all butting in and sticking their noses in your business."

Jed dragged his gaze over to Xander, who jabbed his finger at the driveway and told the driver where to turn. "You know what?" he said. "All of you seem to have forgotten that you've married some pretty terrific women —ones I'm rather partial to, considering they're family. Tom, I'm sure your problem can be solved with nothing more than you giving your wife the attention she evidently needs and evidently is missing. Xander, afraid there's not much I can do about Neil, but marrying Cat meant you got him too. Steven, glad you and Katy are together, and there are worse places to raise Fletcher. The ranch is big enough. You'll figure it out."

All this young love… Jed didn't think he and Diana had ever gone at each other like this. Then there were his boys. Mark was just finishing school, and Jed didn't have a clue what direction he was leaning toward or where his head was. Chris and Danny still had spots to carve out on his land for their wives and his grandbabies, but all either had done was mark out the spot to build more than two years earlier. Maybe here, away from home, he could sit down with all of them and get a sense of where their heads were.

The driver pulled up to the front of the house and parked. The driveway was empty, and everything looked quiet.

"You know, they could be gone," Jed said as Tom pulled open the side door and stepped out.

Xander tossed Jed a look over his shoulder as he opened his door. "We could have passed them, too," he said.

"Maybe," Jed said. "Only one way to find out." He climbed out after Steven and then poked his head back in to address the driver. "Hey, just hang tight. We don't expect to be long. You can leave the meter running, and one of these three will pay the extra tip."

"Si, senor, I'll wait," the driver said and flashed a smile, all white teeth, as he turned off the van.

"Hey, it's locked," Tom called out. He was pressing the bell, and they could hear the ringing from outside. It was quite the echo. He'd expected to hear something, but he took in how quiet the place was. Tom pounded with his fist on the door. "Becky!" he shouted.

Yeah, he was pissed and evidently hadn't heard a word Jed had said. Apparently, he intended to continue butting heads with his wife. Great! Jed considered whether he should give Brad a heads-up about that.

"You know what? I think they may be gone," he called out as he strode to the front door.

Then he thought he heard something. Xander and Steven were talking, and Tom stepped away from the front door, shaking his head. Jed cocked his head, stepping over to the french doors, which were closed. The heavy curtains were drawn, something he'd never seen before. Whatever he'd heard had come from there.

"What is it?" Xander asked as he moved closer to him. He just turned his head and took in how quiet the place was. It was odd, was all he could think.

"Nothing," Jed said. "I guess I thought I heard something. Just don't ever remember it being so quiet, so closed up."

Steven and Tom were already walking back to the minivan, where the driver was waiting for them. The windows were all down, and the heat and humidity had beads of sweat running down Jed's back, under his arms. He couldn't wait to get back to the pool.

"They're probably already back at the resort, by the pool, where we should be right now," he said and rested his hand on Xander's shoulder to pat it before taking a step to the van.

"Tom, help…!"

He heard the scream—Becky, he thought. The group

turned and froze just as a shot fired, and then all hell broke loose.

Xander grabbed him and had him running. Tom turned to the house and was fighting off Steven, who was trying to tackle him and take cover. There was another pop, and glass shattered. Jed felt the bite of it piercing his cheek, and somehow, he grabbed Tom along with Steven and Xander, and they were around the van on the ground.

All he could do was wonder what the hell they had just walked into.

Six

The cab driver was on the ground behind the van, and Xander and Steven were putting everything they had into holding down Tom, who was unbelievably strong.

"Let go of me!" he yelled, struggling to pull away. "Shit, that was Becky. Becky!"

Jed was looking around, seeing the plants, the trees, the driveway behind them, and trying to figure out what to do, trying to get his brain to catch up with the adrenaline pounding through his veins. What the fuck was going on? What was his family stuck in? All he could do was squat behind the van, the only protection between him and the horror on the other side.

"Jed, get the fuck back!" someone yelled. "Don't come any closer…"

It was Neil. Jed was about to stand when Xander grabbed his arm and said, "Get the fuck down! You're hit —your face."

Jed wiped his cheek, seeing blood on his hand, but he felt nothing. His adrenaline was still pumping.

"Neil, what the fuck is going on?" he shouted back. "Who's shooting?" He peeked through the back window of the van, but he heard nothing further, not from Neil. No one else said a word.

Then the french doors opened, and Emily stepped out only partially. He could see blood covering her faded short-sleeved shirt, her hair a mess, and she didn't move any farther. He had to fight the urge to run out and over to her.

"Jed, is Tom here?" she called. Shit, she sounded scared. "We heard Tom... Tom, we need you. Becky needs you. She's hurt."

"I'm here, right here!" Tom yelled, already on his feet. So were Xander and Steven, and this time they didn't try to stop him as he moved around the van. Each step he took, Jed couldn't help fearing the worst. All he knew was that there had been gunfire, and none of them knew what they were walking into.

"Emily, what's going on?" Tom called out. "Where is Becky? She's hurt. I heard her scream..."

Jed could see fear and something else he'd never seen before on Emily's face. His chest tightened at how she was standing, her hands up and shaking. Someone else was there. What did they want?

"There are men here," she said. "They have guns. Becky is shot, and Brad..." Her voice caught. "We need Tom. Rodney was hit in the head and is on the ground, and he hasn't woken up. It's bad..."

Tom was now running across the driveway—reckless, stupid. Jed's sick feeling turned into a full-fledged panic attack. Never before had he imagined this happening to them. He'd read about this kind of thing happening to other people all the time, and he'd never been able to imagine the horror those people felt, not until now.

Xander had his phone to his ear, but Jed put his hand up and pulled it away, shaking his head.

"Don't," he said in a low voice, then moved into the open. Steven was behind Tom, also running, when Emily held up her hand.

"No! Go back, Steven. They said just Tom. Turn around, go now."

Then shots fired, hitting the van, and Steven froze and jumped before running back and diving behind it with Jed, Xander, and the driver. The windows shattered. Jed held his arm over his head and brushed off the bits of glass he could feel in his hair as he peeked up again.

"Emily, Becky is shot?" he called out. "What about Brad and my dad? Is my mom in there? What the hell do they want? Tom, you okay? What about Neil and Candy? I need to know how everyone is." He had never felt so helpless. Xander was making his way to the front of the van, on the ground, as if trying to get a better view.

"We're all here," Emily said. "Your mom and dad… Becky is shot in the leg, and Neil's hurt. He was hit in the head. He's not talking or moving. He's unconscious, I think, and one of the men shot Brad when he tried to—" Emily shrieked. He could see a gun at her head, her hands in the air. She was shaking. "Okay, okay…" she pleaded. "He said to leave and not to call the Mexican police or I'll be shot next, then Candy…"

Tom was right there with Emily, his hands in the air. Emily shrieked again, and Jed was sure someone pulled her back inside. A guy appeared in the doorway, pointing the gun straight at Tom. He was tall, with dark hair, wearing a T-shirt, and he had Tom turn around, his hands still in the air. It looked like he was patting him down with one hand. Tom was looking his way. Jed didn't know if he could see him, but his expression said it all. That was exactly how he was feeling.

"Hey, just tell us what you want," Jed yelled. "That's my family in there. Whatever it is, I'll find a way to get it to you."

Tom stepped around the guy and into the house, and the man remained there, gun pointed right at the van, right where Jed was.

"Go on now," he yelled. "You've been told to leave. Tell no one there, little Jed, because if the police show up here, you'll have signed your family's death certificates. I'll start with the women, then your mom, then your brothers, but I'll save your dad for last, since we still have things to work through. So go on now, Jed—back to your wife, your kids. If anyone else shows up here, be forewarned, I will shoot first and won't be asking questions." Then he stepped back into the house and pulled the doors closed.

He slid down to the ground, his legs shaking. Never in his life had he felt this weak and helpless. Xander scooted back from where he'd been lying on the ground at the front of the van, looking out, and Jed took in Steven squatting down beside him, his hand on the van.

"Holy fuck, we have to call the police..." Steven said, his chest heaving just like Jed's.

"No, that guy's right," Jed said. "We don't know how the Mexicans will handle this, and I'm sure as shit not going to put anyone inside at risk. Shit, shit..." Jed wanted to rage and yell. Beside him, the driver was still sitting on the ground, his ass against the tire. The way he was breathing, Jed could see he was scared out of his mind.

"You see this?" Xander held up his phone to Jed, looking far too composed. He had taken a close-up image of Emily, the blood smeared on her shirt and her jeans, her hands. The sight of the gun to her head sickened him.

Behind her was the guy, someone he'd never seen before. So that had been what Xander was doing: taking photos, a lot of them. At least one of them had been thinking.

"And that tells us what, exactly?" Jed said. "We're totally fucked, up shit creek. We've seen the guy, but now what? We still don't know what they want, and we don't know how bad anyone is hurt in there—Becky, my dad, Neil, Brad…" He shook his head and had to press his hand over his chest as all of the last few minutes hit him. This family reunion had turned into a living, breathing nightmare.

"It gives us a photo, a start. This is what I do, Jed. We can't do anything until we know what he wants, and in case you didn't hear him, this is personal."

Jed found himself taking in the cocky son of a bitch who'd married into the family. Right, a private detective. He reminded himself this kid, because to him Xander was exactly that, was already thinking strategically while he was still reeling from the situation.

"Personal?" he said. "I don't get what you're saying. And how…" He couldn't get the image of Emily, fearful and covered in blood, out of his mind. He wondered if he'd ever be able to close his eyes again and not see it. He didn't know what was happening to his family. He should have been the one figuring out what to do, but he just stared at Xander.

"He knew everyone's names," Xander said. "The family. Mind you, he could have learned that from everyone inside, but I don't think so. He talked about you having a wife and kids, and then he called you little Jed…?" Xander shook his head, still holding up the phone with the image of the man with the gun. "You don't recognize him?"

Jed took the phone and swiped through all the images,

trying to wrap his head around what Xander was saying. Even Steven was looking over his shoulder at the photos, taking them in. His expression said everything about how he was feeling.

Jed couldn't figure out what Xander was alluding to. He was Mister Cool himself, seeming far too comfortable and in his element. "I told you already, no, never seen him. Don't know how he knows about us, and why? We're not famous. We're just people."

"It's planned, everything he said, right down to the order he'd shoot," Xander said. "I didn't miss how he left your dad last, said they had business. This isn't some random bad guys breaking in, a home robbery gone bad, with strangers getting caught in the crossfire. This guy knows your dad. This is very, very personal. So no one called you little Jed?"

Jed couldn't wrap his head around the horror of what Xander was saying. His dad was a good guy. He wasn't one of those scumbags who went around lying, cheating, and screwing people. So what happened that this guy had business with his dad?

"We can't leave and just hope these guys let everyone go," Jed said. "God dammit, I've never felt so helpless in all my life… We don't know what this guy wants or how many of them are in there." He pictured everyone back at the resort and knew they were all waiting for them to come back—laughing, drinking, playing, having fun. This was going to crush everyone. He ran his hand over his face, feeling the sting on his cheek, knowing he'd been hit by something as the burn and bite of pain became very real.

"You're right," Xander said. "We're completely blind out here, which is why one of us needs to stay behind and get into the house."

Just then, another gunshot fired.

"They're still out there, Davis! Damn them fuckers. They're just sitting there behind that cab, just waiting for their opportunity to get in here, and that's if the cops aren't already on their way. I knew this was a bad idea. We should leave now."

Neil took in Alan, who was freaking out over by the window, his back against the wall as he pulled the curtain back and peeked out. He was the unstable one, the one Neil was really uneasy about. He paced back and forth like a caged animal. As bad as Davis was, Alan was far more dangerous, as he didn't appear to have an ounce of control. Pure emotion and rage flickered all over his face, and it was a wonder they weren't all dead.

He could hear a phone buzzing and knew it was likely Brad's or his. The ring tones were the same, and the first thing the other guy had done was take Candy, Emily, and Becky's purses and cell phones.

Brad was tipped over on the floor, bleeding, and he couldn't tell where he was shot—shoulder, chest, or lower? The chair Brad was still tied to was blocking his view, and his head throbbed like a son of a bitch from where he'd been bashed with the back of Davis's gun after yelling out to Jed. They'd been about to leave, and Neil had known that was the only way to get them some kind of help.

Brad had tried to launch himself and his chair at Alan, and Neil had only vaguely heard the shot as the gun connected with his head. Emily had cried out. Candy was somewhere behind him. He thought he may have blacked out for a second, as Tom was now inside, over by Becky, and glanced his way.

"Neil, you okay over there?" he called out.

Becky was doing her best not to cry, Neil thought, as Tom looked at her leg. She was holding his arm, and he was saying something, murmuring, "It's okay. I'm going to fix this."

"Yeah, fine," Neil said. His voice sounded odd. "Brad! Tom, is Brad okay? How is Becky doing?"

Alan was back, peering out the window, appearing completely unhinged. Brad groaned, and it was the sweetest sound. He was alive.

"Brad, talk to me. Tell me how you're doing," Tom called out with a doctor's authority. He pulled tighter at the belt around Becky's leg, and she cried out. "I know it hurts, Becky, but you need to be tough so I can make sure you don't bleed out. There's too much blood here. You'll be fine—I'll make sure you are. I need to check on your dad."

Neil just watched Alan and then Davis. His mom had tears streaming down her face, the gag still in her mouth, and his dad was still on the floor, unmoving. Emily was kneeling on the floor behind Brad, now leaning over him.

"Candy," Neil called.

"On the floor behind you. I'm fine," she said, but her voice said otherwise.

"Go check him," Becky said, her voice weak. "Dad, answer us! You scared the shit out of me."

Tom stood up and then froze, hands in the air, as Davis stepped over to him, gun on him.

"Whoa, where do you think you're going there, doc? I said the girl only."

"I need to check Brad. Just let me see how he is. The last thing you want here is anyone dying." Tom took another step and another, gutsy. Then he was on the ground in front of Brad before Davis could tell him no. Brad was still tied to the chair, sideways on the floor.

Davis opened the french doors and fired a shot. Neil jumped, and Becky and maybe Candy screamed. Had someone else he loved been shot?

"Told you to get out of here!" Davis shouted. "I'm going to count to thirty, and if you're not all in that van and out of here by then, I'll finish off the girl. I told you I'm not messing around."

A second later, he heard a vehicle start up and then pull away, which was both a relief and the worst thing ever. They'd be alone now, no one there, but at least Jed would be gone, and Steven, whom he'd also heard. No one else would be hurt, and they'd get word back to everyone, though that could cause more of a problem. At the same time, they needed someone to do something.

Brad was groaning again.

"Yeah, I know it hurts," Tom said, "but you're lucky it went right through."

"Tom, how's my dad?" Becky called out. She was still bleeding, even with the belt around her thigh, and she didn't look good. She was pale, almost gray.

"Shoulder, doesn't look like it hit anything vital. I need some towels, antiseptic. Is there a medical kit in the house, a first aid kit?" Tom was direct, to the point, as he looked up to Davis and then over to Neil. His mom was nodding, trying to talk around that gag.

"Can you take the gag off my mom, please," Neil said.

As Davis stepped over to his mom, he noted something in his expression—maybe surprise at the *please* he had choked out. Now wasn't the time to antagonize the guy, Neil thought. Davis pulled the gag down, and his mom coughed and dragged in a breath. He'd call him sir or mister or anything he wanted, even get down on his knees and beg, if that would save everyone.

"The laundry room cupboard," his mom said. "Above the washer there's an emergency kit, first aid supplies, everything."

Tom stood up, but the gun snapped over to him.

"No, you stay right where you are!" Davis said, then flicked his gun much like an extension of his hand. "Emily, up! Come on, that's right. You're the gopher because you've done as you're told. Your husband didn't, so he's paid the price. Everyone, take note and learn the first time. I'm not a patient teacher. Get the kit, come right back, because if you don't…" He stepped around the sofa, back to the other end, and lifted his gun on Becky.

Of course, Emily shrieked and pleaded, and Neil shut his eyes for a second, wishing he could wake up from this living nightmare. He took in the way Emily nodded, the way she forced herself to swallow. She was trembling. This was a mother's worst fear. Then she was gone. He could hear cupboards banging, and then she was back a second later with a red bag with a white first aid symbol on it and a bunch of his mom's good white towels.

"I need to untie Brad," Tom started, but Davis was already shaking his head.

"No. He's lucky I'm letting you do anything to help him. I'm tempted to just let him lie there and bleed…"

"No, please!" Becky shouted at him. "That's my dad. You're a monster, you're a cold-hearted fucking asshole…"

The way Davis glanced down at her, Neil feared the worst and held his breath for a second, willing her to watch her mouth.

"Davis, she's just a kid," Neil begged. Tom glanced over to him. "She's just had a baby. Leave her be, please. Take it out on me, not her." Then he glanced back to her and snapped, "Becky, watch your mouth."

"Davis, I'm not liking this," Alan said. "You said we would be in and out of here, that it wouldn't take long. It was supposed to be just the old man. You'd get what was owed to you and we'd leave. This is going to shit! Who else is going to show up? How do we know we won't have half the Mexican police and army here surrounding the place? I'm not going back to prison, any prison, but sure as shit I'm not landing in no Mexican hellhole."

Neil couldn't help wondering now which prison he had been in, and for what. "Where did you do time? What did you do?" he asked.

Alan jerked his gaze toward him. Yup, fast coming unglued.

"You sure like to talk," Davis said. "Always did, if I remember. You were the talker, smooth, negotiated your way out of everything. Brad, though, was always trying to be like his daddy, Jed tagging along after both of you. Would've been nice to have little Jed in here too. Be like our own little reunion, catch up, shoot the shit, compare bedtime stories. Bet mine wouldn't have you drifting into a peaceful, carefree sleep."

Brad yelled. All Neil could see was Tom pressing a white towel against Brad's shoulder, and then Emily was holding it for him, and he was pulling gauze and bandages from the kit, unwinding and ripping off a chunk.

"Fuck, you have to be enjoying this, aren't you?" Brad said to Tom. Despite his twisted humor, his voice shook.

"At any other time…" Tom said. "You're going to be okay, but got nothing for the pain. Emily, hold that."

Neil had to force himself to drag his gaze back to Davis, and he wasn't sure what he was seeing in his face, the way he looked at Brad for a second—sorrow, anger, or maybe regret. Neil racked his brain, trying to remember what Davis had been talking about, then shut his eyes.

"Right…Robbie Davis," he said in a low voice. "Robbie, remember that old treehouse we built down in the ravine?"

He had forgotten until now. The memory of that moment had come to him, and he was still trying to get his head around what Robbie had said. He didn't even remember how old he had been, maybe eight. Robbie had been there one day and then gone, the old house empty. Whatever had happened to that house?

"Yup, put together with scraps of wood and branches," Robbie said. "Little Jed was the kicker, dragging branches the size of trees, bigger than him, stubborn little shit, even when you and Brad told him to get lost, to go on home, that he wasn't old enough and this was ours, not his. He was determined, though. Wouldn't take nothing from either of you, working harder than all of us. Is he still that way?"

Neil pulled in a breath, deep, trying to remember what he was talking about. Those were Robbie's memories, not his.

"That's my Jed," his mom said. "Never gave in. Still doesn't." Her voice sounded so dry.

He could hear his dad moaning now, he thought, and Tom moved back to Becky, dragging the bag with him. Brad was lying there on the floor, still tied to that damn chair, a bandage just below his shoulder, his shirt ripped open, dried blood smeared on his chest, bloody towels on the floor. He was awake, though, and looking over to him. Neil could see he was hurting, but he wasn't going to give in.

"Neil, is Rodney waking up there?" Tom called out. He was using the scissors, cutting Becky's jeans and then ripping them open all the way up the leg. Trauma doc in the family—no, the head of trauma. They'd gotten lucky, and Neil prayed Tom was as good as he'd been told.

He turned his head slowly, feeling dizzy and wanting to puke, then pulled in a deep breath to steady the nausea. His dad was on his side still, hands tied behind his back, but he was moving. "I think so," he said. "Dad…"

Robbie stepped over and stood right in front of his dad. Alan was by the stairs, his gun up, watching Tom and then Emily, who was on the floor with Brad, the only one besides Tom and Becky not tied up. Emily had her hand on Brad, and Neil waited until she looked his way, but she just shook her head as if she knew what he was thinking, shutting him down even though he hadn't said one word.

"Come on, wake up," Robbie said. He was squatting down in front of Rodney, and he poked him in the shoulder with the gun.

Neil remembered now what he'd said about the house, the property—his, not theirs. "Robbie, you said it was your house, your property, but I don't remember it that way. I'm not trying to disagree or anything, but I was just a kid, so maybe you could fill me in on what I'm missing."

Robbie pulled his gaze and the gun from Rodney, whose eyes were now open. His head was still bleeding, but some of it had dried. At least Robbie wasn't focusing on his dad with that rage, that anger. Neil knew he wouldn't hesitate to pull the trigger.

"You calling me a liar?" he said and stood up. This could go sideways really quickly.

"No, not at all. I just remember we were friends, always playing together, hanging out. On weekends, after we finished chores around the ranch, we were inseparable. You were there one day, and then suddenly you were just gone. I never knew what happened, just that you weren't there one Sunday. Brad and I waited, and I finally left him at the treehouse and went to your house, but it was empty. The door was unlocked, and only the sofa, a mattress and table were left, everything else was gone. You'd said nothing, not a word. It hurt."

What was it about memories? They had faded, but now they were coming back in bits and pieces after all these years.

Robbie was right in front of him, looking down on him, and he pouted out his lower lip as if mocking him. "Oh, that's quite the memory, so sad. You say it as if I meant something to you." Then he turned, staring down at Rodney. "Did you hear that, old man? Even your son doesn't know what you did, how far you went to get something that wasn't yours. You broke up a family, crushed them like they were nothing but a bug you could step on. Yeah, my dad was never the same after you stole what was his, and because of you, I never got what I was owed."

"Robbie, you've got it wrong…" Rodney started, but Robbie kicked him in the stomach, and he coughed and groaned. His mom cried out. Brad too, he thought, and Emily and Candy.

All Neil could feel and see in Robbie was anger, hurt, betrayal. Whatever Robbie thought had happened, telling him otherwise was only going to get someone killed.

"Don't tell me I got it wrong, you fucking prick," Robbie said. "I've waited my whole life for this moment, to see your face again, to get payback for every punch I got, every cruel word, every night I went hungry…to get what is rightfully mine." He held the gun up and cocked it, and in that second, Neil was positive he was going to shoot his dad.

"Robbie, look," he said, panicked. "I'm not saying my dad is right. I'm not even arguing with you. I was just a kid, and so were you. I just want to hear your side of what happened. My dad never told us, and if he did something like you said he did, stole from you, then you're right, you're absolutely fucking right, there should be payback. But you have to tell me first what happened…"

He didn't pull his gaze from Robbie, seeing the way he stared down at his dad, the hate. He despised him. Neil held his breath, waiting. Finally, Robbie un-cocked the gun and let it fall to his side, and he let out a breath that heaved in his chest. He wondered if everyone had been counting the same seconds and had any idea how very close to the edge they were all standing.

One wrong word, one wrong move, and this whole thing was going to go very, very badly. He was smart, and this was his arena, getting someone to believe they were being heard, but not this way, not ever in a life or death situation where mistakes could have such dire consequences. He had known this man as a boy, but the stranger before him wasn't that same kid.

"Robbie, please…" he added.

Robbie moved his mouth, thinking, and then his gaze landed back on Neil.

"Davis, what the fuck are you doing?" Alan said. "Let's just get the money and get the hell out of here before someone comes back."

The way he was twitching, Neil wondered if it was more than nerves. Drugs, maybe. Was he coming down from a high? That was even worse. Time wasn't really on their side.

"Robbie, come on," Neil said. Was he getting through to him? "I swear to you, I will make it right."

"Okay, enough talking!" Robbie shouted, aiming the gun straight at Neil, right at his face. The eyes staring back at him were filled with a hate he hadn't expected. "First, you're going to sign over the entire property to me, and then you're going to pay for all the years of suffering, the struggle, having everything I loved taken away from me—our home, our land, my dad, my life. And just so we're even…" He turned to Rodney, moving deliberately even though his gun was still levelled on Neil. Nothing in his expression showed an ounce of compassion. This was anger, this was revenge. This was getting his pound of flesh. "You took my dad from me, so I'm going to take one of your sons from you. The thing is, I'm not the cold-hearted bastard you are, so I'm going to let you choose. So which one will it be, Neil or Brad?"

Eight

"Jesus, Steven, stay on the damn road," Jed snapped from the passenger seat. He knew he was sitting on glass, feeling the bite of it through his shorts. His window was blown out, and there were bullet holes in the windshield. Steven was behind the wheel, passing cars and switching lanes, and Jed could barely see where the road was through the cracked glass.

He thought the cabbie in the back was praying from the way he kept muttering on and on. Jed braced his hand against the dashboard as Steven jammed his foot on the gas, driving a little too fast and out of control. The engine was making a god-awful noise, and steam had started to rise from the hood with a hiss. A horn blasted as he swerved from one lane to the next, never pulling his eyes from the road.

"Get us back in one piece and without the cops pulling us over. I'm not about to answer their questions, because that will likely get us hauled in and stuck behind bars, so slow the fuck down!" Jed shouted.

The high rise of the resort was looming ahead, and

Steven was gripping the wheel, the muscles in his arms flexed, pumped. Jed thought he gave it a little more gas.

"Like, what the fuck? What the fuck?" Steven yelled, slapping the wheel again and again as he pulled up to the gates of the resort. Jed took in the security at the front and the shock that they couldn't hide.

"Got it, heard you," he said, though Steven was saying exactly what he'd been saying over and over in his own mind. His heart was still slamming in his chest, his adrenaline still pumping. The tires squealed as Steven slammed the brakes, pulling up behind another cab from which people were getting out. Jed damn near went through the windshield, and he wondered whether he'd be picking glass shards out of his ass.

The cabbie was at the side door, yanking on it, and Jed rested his hand on his shoulder. The man's eyes were still freaked out as they locked on to his.

"Remember," Jed said, "we don't know who shot at us. That's all you say."

The cabbie nodded frantically. Jed should have learned his name. *Luis* was all his nametag read, still pinned sideways to his shirt. Yeah, he was scared shitless. "Si, senor, of course," he stammered as he pulled on the side door and opened it.

Jed stepped out and took in the way Luis ran into the hotel, hoping he'd get the story straight. One of the mangers ran over along with a couple others, taking in the van and asking if they were okay and what had happened.

Jed wasn't listening. None other than Neil's son, Michael, was getting out of the car in front of him, and his eyes widened as he took in Jed and then Steven, who came around the front of the van.

"What the…" was all Michael said. A gorgeous blond woman was with him—had to be his wife. What was her name again? Jed couldn't remember. He was doing his damnedest to keep it together.

"Senor Friessen, I'm so sorry," one of the managers said, hurrying out of the resort. He was the last person Jed wanted to talk to. "I just heard bandits shot at you."

"Yeah, yeah—sorry, I don't know. We didn't see anything, just bullets flying. I don't even know where we were," he rattled off.

Michael's jaw slackened, and Jed thought he was going to ask more, but he just gestured to Jed's face. "You have blood on your cheek," he said. "You were hit? You need a doctor."

Jed put his hand on his arm and turned him to the hotel, realizing as he walked that he had only one flip-flop on. His other foot was bare. Steven was already through the lobby doors, and there were people coming out, looking at him and the van. He could hear the hiss of voices behind him, and the last thing he wanted was a swarm of questions.

"Let's go," he said in a low voice, holding Michael's arm because his legs were now shaking like a son of a bitch. "We need to talk, but not here. Something happened."

Maybe Michael understood, as he was leading the way, the blonde hurrying beside him and pulling the door open, holding it. Jed walked through, keeping his head down as they moved down the hall and cut across the courtyard to their bank of rooms on the other side. Ahead, Steven turned the corner into the lush greens and coconut trees that led out to the pools. He was talking, gesturing wildly to Andy and Mark, who was also there. Both were in swimsuits

Jed started toward them, and they lifted their gazes to him. Mark rested his sunglasses on his reddish hair. Steven was freaking out, and Andy and Mark stared at him in shock.

"Dad, like…" Mark started.

"Enough, not here," Jed said. "Andy, we've got kind of a situation, so let's go talk in the room—like, with everyone."

Andy just blinked, taking in the arrival of Michael, as well. "Where're Xander and Tom?" he finally asked.

Mark took another step closer to him, long and lanky, with his mother's piercing blue eyes, but he was the spitting image of Jed at his age. "Holy crap, Dad. Your face is bleeding. You were hit?"

What could he say? Evident, Steven had already told them some of what had happened, but Jed had no fucking idea how or when he had been hurt, as he'd been diving for cover while bullets flew. He was alive and in one piece. That was all that mattered.

"Oh, good, you're back," said Cat as she approached, carrying Nathan. "Is Xander in the room? I expected my dad to track me down already and take the baby…" She stopped, and her eyes widened, the odd blue. She must have figured out then that there was a problem. Jed hadn't glanced in a mirror, and he had to look pretty bad, by the way everyone kept staring at him.

"What happened?" Cat came closer and looked around. "Where's Xander?"

Steven dragged his gaze back to Jed, who knew he was waiting for him to tell her.

"Well, that's the thing we need to talk about," Jed said. "We've got a problem, and Xander figured he was the best person to stay behind."

"You know Diana is going to freak when she sees you," Andy said to him as Steven tapped the key card he'd taken from Mark against the door of his family's suite over and over, but nothing happened. Jed thought he was going lose it as he finally kicked the door and yelled, "Fuck!"

"Hey, hey, hey," Andy said. He stepped past Jed and took the key card from Steven just before the door was yanked open.

"What is going on?" Diana shrieked.

Steven went inside first, and Jed felt a hand on his back, prodding him forward. He knew it was Michael, or maybe Mark, as Andy stepped inside. Diana stared at him with horror, and he saw Katy at the island in the kitchen, cutting up carrots. Steven had already pulled a beer from the fridge, twisted the top off, and was downing it.

The door closed, and he caught a glimpse of his face in the mirror over the desk. There was blood down one side from a cut. From what, he didn't know.

"Diana, do you mind if I borrow…?" JD stopped in the doorway from one of the bedrooms. On her hip was Sophia, his three-year-old granddaughter. JD took one look at him, and her eyes widened.

"We have a situation. It would be best if everyone was here," Jed said. Andy and Michael stood in the middle of the dining area.

"So where is Xander, exactly?" Cat said. "You said he stayed behind to handle…what? You went to Gramma and Grampa's, but where are my mom and dad?"

Michael's wife was now holding Nathan. Michael had yet to say anything, just staring at Jed.

"Yes, we were at the estate," Jed said. "We went there and…he stayed behind. He's there now." Good God, he was rambling, talking in circles.

Steven slammed his beer bottle on the island beside

Katy and rested both his hands there, leaning as if he was having trouble getting air, before he slapped the counter again with both hands. "There were guns and bullets flying, and, holy shit, Becky is shot, and Rodney is hurt. How bad, who the fuck knows? Brad too, maybe, and Neil. We don't know a fucking thing, just that some goddamn fucking sickos—"

"Steven," Jed said, trying to cut through his freak-out. Diana was in front of him, touching his face with a wet cloth. Damn, it stung. He hissed. "We don't know anything except that Tom stayed. They let Tom in, and the whole fucked-up scenario…I still don't get it."

"What about the police?" Diana said. "Are they there?"

Jed just stared at his wife, seeing the shock on everyone's faces as he shook his head. "They said no police. Considering the situation, the Mexican authorities could shoot first and ask questions later."

"My mom and dad, and Becky? You said she's shot?" Katy cried, stepping around the island and jamming her hands in her hair. "Call the police right now!"

Andy was talking to someone on his cell phone, and Michael and Cat had yet to say a word.

"That was Laura. Everyone is on their way up," Andy said. "I'm not sure I understand, Jed. You said gunmen were at the estate. What do they want? There was shooting?"

Jed couldn't pull his gaze from the hurt and agony he saw in Katy. Steven must have figured it out, as he pulled himself together enough to put his hand on her shoulder. "We don't know for sure," he said, but he knew that wasn't going to be enough.

"You said my dad is hurt—shot?" Cat said. Michael rested his hands on her shoulders. Jed wasn't sure what passed between the siblings as he dragged his hand over his forehead again.

"Why is this happening?" Diana said. "I mean, there has to be a reason. This doesn't make sense. Of course you need to call the police. Call them now." She looked at him, at Andy, at all of them.

All Jed could do was shake his head. "No," he said, going to reach for his phone in his pocket, but it wasn't there. Damn, he must have dropped it. "Steven, Andy, one of you text Xander. All I can tell you is when we pulled in, Tom was at the door first, and it was locked. He rang and pounded on the door, calling for Becky…"

"Tom shouted because he was fucking mad at Becky," Steven interrupted. Everyone's eyes were glued on him. "We were walking back to the van because the place was all closed up and looked deserted, and then we were shot at. We dived behind the van, the bullets were flying, and then Emily came out…" He stopped talking, and Jed hoped it was because he realized no one needed to hear that Emily had blood all over her shirt.

"And what?" Michael said "I'm totally out of the loop here. Like, why?"

Jed rubbed his hand over his face. "Emily came out with a message. There was a gun on her. She asked for Tom because Becky needed help. She said Becky had been shot, and Neil and my dad were hit or something, unconscious maybe. Brad…she didn't tell us if he was shot or what, so of course I'm thinking the worst. Then one of the men came out with a gun and patted Tom down as if checking for weapons. Emily said nothing about Candy or my mom. Xander did manage to get a photo of the gunman, but we don't know how many are there or what they want. The guy knew information about us, so Xander thinks this could be personal, not some random situation."

Jed gestured wildly. Across the room, Mark was leaning against the wall, and the sight of his son kept Jed focused.

No one was saying a word, just taking everything in. At the door, a key card clicked the lock, and there were voices in the hall. It looked like Laura had dragged everyone up.

"Got something," Andy said to Jed, holding over his phone. It was a text from Xander with a photo from what looked like inside the house, followed by a text.

Everyone alive. Becky shot in leg. Brad shot in shoulder. Sometimes I don't like being right, but this is personal.

Nine

Xander was in Rodney and Becky's room, having made his way around the house to the back, where he'd climbed the shaky metal trellis to the balcony and pulled himself up over the rail outside the unlocked door. That was something he would speak to Rodney and Becky about, if they all made it out alive. Security was what he did, and this place was lacking alarms, locks, and maybe cameras too.

He pulled the door closed behind him. There was something about sneaking into a house. Every sound he made, he wondered if anyone had heard. He could hear muffled voices from downstairs, and he waited where he was before pulling open the door of the bedroom to listen for any voices upstairs. Nothing. Gently, quietly, he slipped into the hall, staying close to the wall as he made his way to the stairs.

He stayed in the shadows behind a potted fern and pulled on all his senses, hearing everything, trying to get a sense of what was going on. He was still reeling and trying to make sense of why the men were there, what they wanted. The facts as he knew them were that a debt was owed, and Robbie Davis had known Jed, Brad, and Neil as boys. It was about property, money, and an eye for an eye. Someone was going to get killed.

He had to fight the panic. *Take a breath. Listen.*

There were two men, one of whom sounded erratic. Tensions were high, and everyone was scared.

So Neil was hurt? Probably because of his big mouth, Xander mused, but at the same time, he had to give him points for his fast talking. That could be the thing that saved them, considering even he was starting to believe Neil would make things right and really did want to know the truth of what had happened.

Did Xander wonder what Rodney had done way back when? Hell, yes, but he also knew from all his investigating that everyone had a past. No one was squeaky clean, and not a person out there had done nothing they wished they could go back and undo. Maybe he didn't want to know, considering Rodney was his wife's grandfather, and he liked him.

He still didn't know how bad off Becky was, but he had heard Tom say she was shot in the leg, and Brad in the shoulder. He thought Rodney was awake, and he could hear the fear, the tension, the yelling, the crying. Everyone downstairs was scared shitless, and he was scared for all of them.

He'd listened to the old man being kicked, and it had taken everything in him to stay where he was after getting a photo of the second gunman. He just wished he could see into the living room to get a better idea. His only source of communication with those back at the resort was Andy, via text. He didn't like what he was feeling, and it took everything he had to keep his head from going to the worst-case scenario.

Just assess. Figure out where everyone is, he had to remind himself over and over. Without a plan, someone would end up dead.

"I need to get her to the hospital," Tom said. "For God's sake, man, she already has an infection setting in. The bullet is still in her leg, she's in a lot of pain, I can't stop the bleeding…"

"No one leaves," Davis said. "You're a doctor. You fix her up. You have a first aid kit. Come on, get creative. Doctors in less civilized countries work with less."

He was cocky, arrogant, and unbending, but he was angry. Xander could hear it in his tone. He would have bet that neither of the men downstairs had anything to lose. Yeah, this wasn't just a dangerous situation. This was dire.

"Look, the longer the bullet stays in, the more the infection sets in," Tom said. "She's still bleeding, and although it's tied off, she's losing too much blood. She needs surgery, which I can't do here. She needs a sterile hospital, medicine, and—"

"Hey, I told you you're not leaving. Fix her or don't fix her. Keep in mind, the longer it takes for me to get what I want, the longer this goes on and she bleeds to death."

"You said you want the ranch signed over?" Brad said, though he didn't sound good. "Fine, do it. Give me a pen…"

Xander looked at the stairs, seeing the door open to the den. If he could just get down there, he knew it led to the dining room and then the kitchen, but even from the den, he would have a better view. A better view meant a better chance of figuring out how to end this.

Someone was crying. He thought it was Rodney. It was horrible, listening.

"Look, Robbie," Neil said. "The ranch, money, you got it, but have you thought about how you're going to get out of here, how you'll get out of Mexico? You want the ranch signed over to you, but getting the deed to the property isn't as easy as Brad signing it over. It takes a lawyer, a banker, some calls…" Neil was really working the situation, but at the same time, Xander wondered if he'd go too far.

"Some calls, you mean to the police, the army, a bunch of security who'll kick down the door?" The man laughed. "The first bullet will be in you."

Xander didn't have a clue what he meant, but he knew sitting up there wasn't going to end this any time soon. Becky needed help, and how bad off was Brad? Yeah, he had to get down the stairs, and maybe he could figure out a way to at least draw one of them out. Could he disarm him? Maybe.

Xander crouched and stayed low as he moved his foot around the plant to the stairs, but he kicked something with his sneaker and heard a crash, a shatter, and quickly pulled back his foot. What the hell was on the stairs, a vase?

He froze for a second, holding his breath, hearing voices.

"Who's up there? You come out right now." Yeah, it was Davis.

Xander moved back, hearing footsteps on the stairs, two at a time. He slipped back into Becky and Rodney's room and heard doors crash open down the hall.

"Come out, come out, wherever you are! Last chance, you little fucker, whoever you are, because if you make me keep looking for you, I'll find you and I'll shoot you, and then I'll kill someone else downstairs just because."

Xander hurried back to the french doors and stepped out, closing them as quiet as he could, knowing anyone could see him there, so he climbed over the rail and held on, trying to reach the trellis with his foot. He couldn't get hold. There was someone in the room, coming his way. He had a second to figure out a way to get down as he looked, seeing the drop, fifteen or maybe twenty feet, and knowing there was no choice.

He let go and dropped to the ground, rolling just as he heard the door open above. He was on his feet and darted around the corner, around the house and into the bushes, where he just waited, listening, knowing Davis was out there on the balcony, watching but not saying a word.

"I know you're out there, you little shit. Whoever you are, show yourself right now or I'll shoot the girl, and that will be on you."

Xander pulled out his phone and could see dozens of texts from Andy, wanting to know what was going on. *Trouble,* he replied. *Could use some help. Two guys with guns. They want land, the ranch. He plans to kill Brad or Neil. They found me. No choice. Have to turn myself in or they'll kill Becky or someone else.*

He dropped his phone in the dirt and grabbed two handfuls, running it over his face and shirt as he stepped out of the bushes, his hands in the air. "Okay, okay! Don't shoot, please, please, senor. I'm just the gardener," he said in his best accent. Davis was on the balcony, aiming his gun at him as he summoned the best performance of his life. "Please don't shoot, senor. I have a little boy, a wife. I'm just a nobody."

He didn't know what Davis was thinking as he stared at him and then nodded. Had he passed, or was he dead?

"You hear anything?" Davis said. "You were in the house. Why were you in the house if you're the gardener?"

Xander shook his head. "Upstairs, sir, hiding. I'm sorry. I was in the bathroom when I heard the commotion. I panicked and was hiding. I just want to go home."

Davis lifted the gun, aiming it right at him. "Yeah, but

the thing is, you seen too much, heard too much. Now what am I supposed to do with you?"

He swallowed, realizing this was it. He imagined Cat and Nathan and felt a horrible ache in his chest.

Then Davis un-cocked the gun and lowered it. "Consider this your early Christmas present. Go on before I change my mind."

Andy was crowded along with everyone into the living room of the penthouse suite, which had three bedrooms, a large kitchen with an island, and a huge oversized balcony with a hot tub. This was one of the four suites, the one where Jed and his family were staying. The three other identical suites were for Brad, Neil, and Andy and their families, but right now they were together, trying to make sense of this nightmare.

All the kids, Ally, Sophie, Gilly, Shaunty, Brandon, Fletcher, and baby Nathan, were in the master bedroom with Elizabeth and Angie, watching a movie, he thought, or playing games or something. Jack, a surly teenager who was looking more and more like Brad every day, refused to go anywhere and was sitting wide-eyed and shocked on the sectional between Diana and Zac. Jasmine and Trevor were in Brad's room. Last someone checked, they had been watching a Star Wars marathon, and Andy had no intention of dragging two autistic adults into the middle of a situation even he didn't want to be in.

Mark, Danny, Evie, JD, Chris, Steven, and Katy were

sitting on the bar stools and leaning against the kitchen island, and everyone was talking. Cat, Sara, Chelsea, Laura, and Tiffy had pulled out the dining room chairs. All he could hear was a low hum in the room, but at the same time, he wasn't listening to a word anyone was saying.

Michael was pacing and on edge. Ric and Jeremy were both leaning against the fireplace, and neither had said a word. After Diana had tried to clean up Jed's face, which had a nice gash that Andy thought could use stitches, Jed had finally gone to change, saying he had glass in his shorts. His legs had scratches, likely also from the glass.

Andy swore everyone was still in shock after hearing everything Jed and Steven had said.

"So Xander's in the house. How did he get in?" Michael asked. "And my mom and dad, how are they? So this is personal, in what way? What do they want?"

Everyone else had stopped talking. That was the question they were all asking as Andy took in Xander's last text.

Jed was in the fridge, and he yanked out a bottle of water, unscrewed the cap, and took a swallow. Andy could see how undone he was. The last he'd heard from Xander was the update he wasn't going to share with anyone—that the gunman wanted an eye for an eye, Brad or Neil killed. There wasn't a chance in hell he was going to say anything with Katy, Steven, and Jack here, and Cat and Michael. Jed, he thought, would be out the door and over there if he heard that.

"I don't know," Andy said. "All we know is it's personal. Xander texted from the house, and everyone is alive, so that's good. At the same time, we need to come up with a plan, something viable that's going to fix this."

"Okay, sure," Katy said, "but my sister is shot, and my dad too. We need to call the police, get them in there, and they can do what cops are supposed to do and—"

"And what, Katy?" Jed snapped. "Do you forget where we are? This isn't a matter of calling the good guys to come in and save the day. It doesn't work like that down here. This is Mexico, and you forget we're guests here. This isn't our country. The same laws don't apply."

Maybe Jed was being a little rough, and Diana must have known, as she went over to him and rested her hand on Jed's shoulder and said something. He just shook his head and said, "No, we need to figure something out. It just doesn't make sense. It was personal…"

There was banging on the door. They all froze, and Danny, who was closest, opened it a crack and then pulled it all the way open. It took Andy a second to recognize Xander under all the dirt on his face and shirt. Cat jumped up and was in his arms.

"Holy shit, Xander!" Michael yelled. "What the hell? I thought you were in the house. How's my mom, dad, everyone…?"

Xander just shook his head and stepped into the room, taking Cat with him, who had her arms over his shoulders and around his neck. He just lifted her, and she didn't let go as he kissed the side of her head.

"I was…" He was breathing heavy and sweating, beads running down his face with the dirt. It was turning to mud. "I climbed the trellis, made it into your grandparents' room," he said to Cat, then looked over to Andy and Jed, who walked around the island and was nearly in his face. "I was at the top of the stairs. Tom is in there, and he's taking care of your dad and Becky. Everyone's alive. Your granddad woke up and was talking."

Andy looked over to Katy and Jack, who were sitting so quiet.

"Neil is trying to negotiate…" Xander started, but Cat

cried out, and Michael shut his eyes a second. Andy was pretty sure it was relief.

"Dad's okay?" Cat said.

"Yeah, he sounded okay. There's no better negotiator. He's convincing, and if I know your dad, he can talk his way into them surrendering. But as I texted you, Andy, they want land, the ranch, and payback. This is personal. It's just the one guy, Robbie Davis…" He gestured to Andy. "Someone write this down. I dropped my phone and had to leave it in the bushes when he let me go. It's only two guys with guns. The other guy, called Alan, is just along for the ride, as back-up. Don't know what he was promised, and I don't know if they have more weapons, ammunition, or what. Everyone is in the living room. I do know that much. I was about to get downstairs to the den when I kicked something on the stairs. It shattered, they figured out someone was in the house, and I got out and over the rail and was hiding, but he knew I was there. I had no choice but to come out, as they were going to kill someone, so I covered myself in dirt and pretended to be the gardener." Xander pulled one of Cat's arms from around his neck, but she didn't step back.

"So he just let you go because he thought you were the gardener?" Steven said, sounding pissed.

"Apparently he has a soft spot for those with nothing," Xander said. "There's more: Davis knew you all as kids, Jed, Neil, and Brad. He said something about a house and property that Rodney stole from his dad."

Andy couldn't believe what he was hearing. Someone gasped, and there was something in Jed's expression, the way he stared at Xander. Andy could see he was thinking or maybe remembering something.

"Robbie Davis," Jed said. "Neil's age, I think. Yeah, yeah…he used to call me little Jed. I haven't thought of him in years. He and his dad lived in that old house that isn't there anymore at the east edge of the ranch."

Andy had a sick feeling.

"Well, that's the thing," Xander said. "From what I heard, he seems to think the ranch is his."

"So let me get this straight," said Danny, finally adding his two cents after sitting quietly and taking it all in. "There are two men with guns at Gramma and Grampa's, and it's turned violent. Becky is shot, Brad and Grampa are hurt, and so is Uncle Neil, all because of something Grampa may have done?"

Chris was shaking his head, his arms crossed, and for a minute Andy thought he was going to add something.

"We don't know that he did anything," Jed said, but the way Xander was looking over to him, Andy wondered if that was true. If they had been talking about his dad, Todd, the question would be what he *hadn't* done.

"So what are we supposed to do, sit around and discuss this some more?" Mark cut in. "I say we go over there…"

It looked like Jeremy was about to agree, but Jed shut him down, saying, "We're not running in there and getting our asses shot off, because that'll get someone killed inside. So cool it."

Ric lifted his hand. "There is another way, you know," he said.

Andy took in his son-in-law, who likely had an idea of the kind of people they were dealing with but who'd said nothing until now. "Well, any ideas are welcome," he said, allowing his gaze to take in his kids, his cousins kids, his family. "Right now, it's not sounding like we're dealing with the most reasonable people who are going to let anyone just walk away. I'm open to anything except anyone else walking into the line of fire."

The idea of losing a huge part of their family—Brad

and Emily, his aunt and uncle, Neil and Candy, and then Becky and Tom…it would be too much. Maybe Jed understood a little of what he was thinking by the way his gaze drifted over to him.

"We give them what they think they want," Ric said and shrugged, stepping away from the fireplace.

"And how do we know what that is?" Jeremy piped in.

Xander still had his arm around Cat. "First, and I'm pretty sure I'm following what you're saying, Ric, we find out the truth of what happened. But be prepared, because it may not be a truth you want to know."

CHAPTER

Eleven

Brad was reeling. Someone had been in the house.

He was still stuck on what Robbie Davis had said about the poor gardener who'd been hiding upstairs. To show he wasn't a heartless bastard, he'd let him go. Let him go, as if he were this amazing hero. Except the problem was that Brad knew his mom didn't have a gardener. Had she hired someone new? No, the way she hesitated when Davis told them about the young and dirty man had confirmed it. So who had it been?

Brad didn't have a clue, and he wasn't about to stop and ask what the man looked like. He just hoped some kind of help was on the way as he listened to Robbie preaching as if standing at a pulpit. Brad was very aware that each of them was completely at his mercy. He was still keeping watch over his daughter and knew from Tom's expression that her situation was dire.

"This is the dirt of family secrets," Davis said, "the legacy that has been passed down for generations, from one to the next, the sins of the father. Your father stole from us, from me and my father, who were powerless to fight back. No, we were just gone. That was the power of a man with money and the force of law behind him. You wanted something that wasn't yours, and my father said no, but that wasn't enough. So now here we are, all these years later, and I'm here to take back what's rightfully mine, plus interest for all the pain and suffering I endured. Right now, this here gives me the power." Davis cocked the gun as he pointed it at Rodney, then un-cocked it again, too comfortable. "I've waited over forty years for my chance."

Brad dragged his gaze over to Neil, who was as helpless as him, tied up. Candy was on the floor behind him, her hands and feet tied. He couldn't see her face but knew she had to be as scared out of her mind as all of them were. His heart pounded, and he found it hard to pull in a deep breath while Davis toyed with his dad, messed with all of them.

"You know not a day has gone by that I haven't thought about you, what you stole," Davis said. "My hate for you is what's kept me going. I lived every single day for this moment, just waiting for that taste of payback, of justice, seeing you under my mercy. How does it feel, old man?"

Brad had to struggle to keep his eyes open even with the sharp, shooting, burning pain in his shoulder. The bullet had gone right through, Tom had said, which was hard to believe. Brad had never been shot before, though, and to make it worse, the cramping in his arms and shoulders was reaching a point of intolerable agony. Though Tom had righted the chair, Brad's hands were still tied behind his back.

His contentious relationship with Tom seemed so irrelevant now when he was the one saving his daughter, doing what he could for her. Emily was sitting on the floor, leaning against him. His mom looked rough, and he wondered how much more she'd be able to take. Robbie Davis was a cruel man, and the way he stood over his dad, pointing the gun at him over and over, Brad feared it was only seconds before he'd put a bullet in him or his daughter or someone else he loved.

"Robbie, I told you, you have it wrong," Rodney choked out. "Maybe I didn't handle it like I should have, but I have nothing I wasn't entitled to."

Davis laughed. "I guess that's the problem: this entitlement you feel. Does that include lying, cheating, and stealing to have the upper hand? Because that's exactly what you did. I guess if you already have something, if you have the means, the money, a bigger property, influence in the county, that excuses you taking what wasn't yours…"

"Robbie, Neil and I are at a loss," Brad said. "You keep saying that our dad stole from you, the house you lived in on the east side of the property. You keep saying that was yours…"

"It was our property, me and my dad! It was our house, a small piece of land. It was tiny in comparison to the massive acres your dad owned, which surrounded it, but it was ours, our home, my roots, and today it would be mine," he snapped, turning on Brad.

Brad looked over to Neil, who was watching him. He could see his brother was trying to figure out how to reason with Davis, but Neil also didn't look good, likely from getting hit in the head with the gun. Brad couldn't figure out a way to talk this guy down. He'd already said he'd sign the ranch over to him, give him anything, but he was still there. Then there was the fact that Davis wanted an eye for an eye, either Neil or him dead.

"Okay, let's say for argument's sake you're right," Brad said. "I'm not saying my dad's lying or that you are. What

I'm saying is that property is mine now, and this is the first I'm hearing about any of this. I guess I always thought you and your dad lived there when it was our land. I don't know what happened. The house is long gone. I don't even remember when it was torn down…"

One day it had been there, the next it had been gone. His dad had said it was an eyesore and he had plans for that spot, but those plans must have never come to fruition, because it was now just a grassy knoll on the hill where the cattle grazed. His dad had said nothing of it until now.

"It would be helpful if we could get your dad on the phone," Brad said. "I'd like to hear from him what happened. As I said, I'll sign the ranch over to him and you…"

Davis was already shaking his head. "Kind of hard, considering that was what killed my dad, having something he loved, that land, our home, taken from him. It killed him because we had nothing, so he gave up. We had a truck, a tent. He put a gun to his head and pulled the trigger. I was ten, and I found him after coming back with an armload of sticks to start a fire where we'd camped after being run out by your father."

Just hearing about it, Brad could see the pain, the hurt of the memory that filled Robbie Davis's expression, along with a fire that could kill all of them. That kind of rabid emotion never ended well. His dark eyes were filled with such hate, not just for his dad but for all of them.

"I'm so sorry," Neil said from where he sat. "I didn't know about your dad. What happened to you?"

His brother really did have a way of making people believe he was truly hearing them and that what they had to say mattered, that he cared. How had Brad not noticed before how he'd mastered the art of conversation?

"You mean after I sat with my dad's dead body, willing

him to wake up? Oh, I suppose after the shock wore off, I walked to town, back to Hoquiam. I don't even know how long it was, really. Hours or a day later. I knew we weren't meant to go back there, fearing the warning your dad had given to my old man: Do not ever set foot back in this town. Those were your words, old man, words I'll never forget. I was a scared-shitless ten-year-old when you stood in our kitchen. I was sitting there, taking everything in, when you said you'd have him arrested on all kinds of charges, get him locked up until he was an old man. As a terrified little kid, I walked back into Hoquiam, right back into that town I was not welcome in, thinking I'd be tossed in jail because I had disobeyed. Someone found me, and I don't even remember what I said, because the sheriff and others went out to that spot in the woods, and next thing I knew, a woman was telling me I would be put somewhere safe."

Brad was trying to understand what Davis was saying. He found himself looking over to his dad on the floor, whose eyes were squeezed shut. He appeared to be crying. Had he really said all that?

"I'm so, so sorry, Robbie," Neil said. "I had no idea. That's horrible. No kid should have to live through that. Where did you go?"

Davis slowly lifted his gaze. For a second, Brad thought he was reliving a memory. Then he seemed to pull himself together. "Into foster care, the first of twelve homes. Not somewhere safe. I learned pretty quick that foster care is cruel and unfair, and that's aside from being unwanted. You love your children, Brad, Neil?"

"Of course I do, more than my next breath," Brad breathed out.

"Well, it's different in foster care. Any idea what it does to a kid, being unloved, not wanted? It fucks with your head, even in the places where you get to eat, where you're not abused."

There was something about this sick feeling of starting to doubt someone he loved. Had his dad done something, or was this just the misunderstanding of a little boy who'd been through the worst? Brad tried to feel sorrow for Robbie, the boy, but what he was doing to them, to his daughter, who was innocent, was beyond forgivable. Two wrongs did not make a right.

Tom was holding Becky's wrist, looking at his watch and shaking his head, and Brad knew it was bad. "Okay, look," Tom said, furious. "I need to get my wife to a hospital. I've done all I can. I've patched up the hole, but the bullet is still in her, and I know it's nicked a vein. I can't get it out here without risking her bleeding out. She needs surgery, an operating room, and I don't have the equipment. The longer we sit here while you play this game, my wife is the one who pays the price. She's going to die."

Brad knew he needed to find a way to end this, something to agree to so he could get his daughter out of there. "You're right, Robbie," he said. "That wasn't fair. That shouldn't have happened to you. You were just a kid, and I'm sure this is too little too late, but we didn't know. We were just kids, too. I'm sorry for what my dad did, for what you believe he did, but aren't you doing exactly the same thing but worse to my daughter, to us?" He should shut up, but he was desperate.

Davis gave him all his attention, the crazed look back in his eyes.

"My daughter needs a hospital," Brad continued. "You have no axe to grind with her. She's innocent in all this, and so is my wife, Neil's wife, and my mom. You need to let them go. I'll stay, and my dad, but let them go—and Neil, too."

Davis raised a brow, and Brad could hear Emily and Neil protesting, but he wasn't about to listen to them, because right now Davis was giving him the floor, and for the first time, it seemed as if maybe he was getting through.

"You said you want the property," Brad said. "I have the property. It's in my name. I'll sign it over. I already agreed to that, but you'll need to let Neil go so he can handle the details. It has to be notarized by a lawyer. Then you want an eye for an eye? I'll give you me."

"No, Brad!" Emily cried out.

"Dad, this is crazy!" Becky yelled, but he could hear how weak she sounded, and Tom… As Brad glanced over to him, his eyes misted. They had never been overly close, but Tom was who his daughter had chosen, and he was doing what he could to save her, to save them. Brad would've given anything to buy more time, to get the chance to bond. He'd never given Tom the same chances as he had Steven, maybe because Tom was more like him than he could admit.

He dragged his gaze back to Davis and he waited, holding his breath. It seemed the man was considering what he was saying.

"Well, well, well, so you have more balls than your dad. Who'd have thought? So you'd sacrifice yourself to save them?"

His chest ached as he thought of his children, his grandchildren, his wife. "Yeah, I would. Let them go. Let's end this before there's nothing left for you to have. If my daughter dies, you get nothing," he added.

Davis inclined his head. "You mean that in good faith?"

"You have me, you have my dad. You'll get what you want," Brad said again, letting his gaze drift over to Neil.

He could see he was having trouble with what Brad was suggesting.

"Sure, but the problem is that blood is thicker," Davis said. "You think if I let Neil and everyone go, they'll simply walk away? No, I'll have more trouble coming down on me. Look at all of you, coming back for a reunion, the whole family, to that fancy resort of yours, Neil. Even if your property, your life is ripped from you the way I lost everything, you have roots. You have kids, grandkids, happy celebrations and a family that has each other's backs. You don't have one idea of what I've been through, of what it means to have nothing the way I did. I was alone. So, in good faith… Nah, I think not. There's no good faith after what your family has caused me."

He made a face. "However, I will let your daughter go with the doc, and of course Neil can go and get the property signed over to me. Even Emily, my gopher…" His expression actually softened as he looked at Emily, who was gripping Brad's leg so hard he wanted to tell her to ease up. "But Neil's wife stays, as does your mother. Sorry about that, Missus Friessen, but you're guilty by association. What your husband did, as far as I'm concerned, you did too by not speaking up, by letting him get away with being a lying, cheating, corrupt human being."

It was more than he expected, and he had to fight the relief that tightened his chest, the ache. He let out a breath that sounded as if it echoed in the room, but he was aware they weren't out the door yet.

"Alan, untie Neil," Davis said.

When Brad flicked his gaze over to his brother, who was being untied, he saw the plea there: *Don't let anything happen to Candy.* He just nodded and dragged his gaze back over to Tom, who lifted Becky in his arms despite her cries from how much she was hurting. Then Brad just took in his wife, who was refusing to move. "Emily, go with Tom and Neil and get Becky to the hospital," he said.

"I don't want to leave you," she whispered. She was going to refuse, now standing in front of him, leaning down, her hands on his face. He took in the tears in her eyes, and for a moment he tried to drink in all of her, knowing this might be the last time he saw her.

"I love you, you know that," he said. "You tell the kids that, too. You are everything, and we've had a good fucking run—the best. I know I'm the luckiest damn asshole for getting you, and I'm so selfish that our time together hasn't been enough, but I need you to get our daughter out of here, for you to get out of here. Our kids need you." He gritted his teeth, having to fight the emotion that threatened to choke him.

Emily pressed her lips to his, hard, desperate, and it killed him, how final it seemed. Then she was pulled away, and she cried out, tears running down her face. He had to drag his gaze over to Tom, who was holding his daughter, as Neil's feet were untied.

"You get my daughter safe, my wife, my family…" His throat thickened. He couldn't get anything else out, because the emotion was something he couldn't hold back. He knew Tom understood what he was saying, and he was having a hard time seeing through the tears that burned his eyes. Maybe Tom was, too. He couldn't tell.

"I will," Tom said. "You know I will."

"Well, enough of this before I change my mind," Davis spat out. He was in front of him and grabbed Emily's arm, and Brad watched as Neil, Emily, and Tom, who was carrying Becky, walked up the three wide steps of the sunken living room. All the while, he listened to Candy quietly sobbing.

Neil grabbed Emily around the waist and actually lifted her when the back door closed and locked. She didn't want to leave Brad any more than he wanted to leave Candy, but this was the only way to save them. His head ached, and just looking into the sun was almost blinding. He had to fight the urge to puke at the wave of dizziness that had hit him the moment he stood up from that chair. He stumbled a bit as Emily slapped at his arm.

"No, Neil, put me down! I can't leave him." She was crying, and Becky was crying too as Tom carried her. He was strong, but he was really struggling.

"Stop it," Neil snapped. "Don't you think I fucking get that? That's my wife in there, too, and I had to leave."

It was enough. She stopped struggling, and they took in the sight of the closed-up garage.

"Fine. I get it, Neil," Emily said. She looked back to the house, but he grabbed her hand and let his gaze linger on her soft blue eyes. There was such an ache there, blurred by tears, a mirror of what he was feeling—but he couldn't allow it, not right now.

"Let's get my dad's car in the garage," Neil said, then turned to Tom, who was handling this better than he was. "There's no way we're going to be able to walk out of here with Becky. It'll take too long."

He hoped there were keys in there. A spare was always kept in the locked cabinet, if he could just get in.

"Neil, we can't just leave my dad there!" Becky cried out as Neil tried the door, but it was locked, of course. It would've been too easy if it was open.

"Becky, I swear to God. I can't sugarcoat anything right now for you. Be a big girl. We can't stay. You need to go to the hospital, and I need all of you to help me get us the fuck out of here, because that's the only thing that's going to save them," he said, then slammed his body against the door. "God fucking dammit!" he yelled. It wouldn't budge, and the dizziness damn near took him to his knees.

"Neil, stop!" Tom said. "Seriously, you're hurt. I can see it from here. You likely have a concussion, and you passing out isn't going to help. Let me put Becky down. I'll work at the door."

Neil took in mother and daughter. Emily had her arm around Becky, who was now on the ground.

"Back up. I'll try kicking it," Tom said.

Neil had to fight a wave of dizziness as he watched Tom ram his foot up in a side kick again and again. The frame splintered, and the door opened. Neil glanced once down to Emily, who just nodded. Becky's leg was wrapped in a thick gauze bandage, and her pant leg was ripped open all the way up. The blood was soaking through the bandage, and Brad's belt was still wrapped tight above where the bullet had hit her.

"Door's unlocked. Where're the keys, Neil?" Tom called out.

Neil followed him in, taking in two vehicles, a white Yukon and a beige two-door Buick. The gun cabinet was next to the cabinet that held the keys, and he touched the latch. He tossed the keys to Tom. "You drive," he said. "Emily, get in."

Tom lifted Becky and eased her into the back seat next to Emily. Neil pressed the garage door opener as Tom closed up the back door and climbed in the driver's side.

"Neil, let's go," Tom said.

Neil took in the gun cabinet. He knew that at least at one point, it had held a rifle and a shotgun, at least four or five guns from his dad's collection. The steel cabinet was always locked, and he listened vaguely as Tom started the SUV. He walked over to the wall of tools and pulled open a steel red drawer, then another.

"Neil, what the fuck? We've got to go," Tom called.

Neil wrapped his hands around a crowbar and walked back to the cabinet, where he jammed the bar under the lock and pried and pulled until he heard it give, and it opened to reveal shells and guns. He grabbed the twelve-gauge semiautomatic. It held five shots, and he took in the boxes of shells stacked at the bottom of the cabinet and loaded some in.

He turned to Tom, and he was pretty sure the young man had an idea of what he was doing as he walked over to the SUV. "Go now," Neil said. "Get Becky to the hospital. I'm staying. I'm not leaving my family in there."

Tom had his hands around the wheel and shook his head. "At any other time, I'd agree with you, but I know you have a head injury, and there's no way this is a good idea. That guy in there is born for this. You're not. Get in the SUV. Let's get out of here and come back after we get

Becky to the hospital, get you and Emily checked out. We need to come back with a plan and with the right kind of help that isn't going to get someone killed."

Neil just shook his head, taking in the wide eyes of Emily and Becky in back, watching him. They were in shock, of course. So was he. He rested his hand on Tom's arm. "I can't," he said. "If it was your wife left in there… and my brother, my parents." He shook his head. He knew what Brad had sacrificed. He'd taken the choice from his dad. He'd saved him.

Tom must have understood, as he gave a single nod and pulled the door closed, then backed out of the garage. Neil just watched him pull away and down the driveway, and he filled the pockets of his jeans with more shells.

He stepped out of the garage, going around the side. He and his dad had built the estate from the ground up. He knew every side door, every window, every way in and out. He'd get back in that house. He may have been born to run the business world, but his father had taught all of them how to shoot—and to never let someone come between them and the people they loved.

Andy didn't know how he'd done it, but he'd managed to talk Laura into keeping all the women in Jed and Diana's penthouse suite while Xander slipped out with Michael, Steven, Chris, Ric, and Danny. In the penthouse suite where Neil and his family had been staying, Xander and Ric were figuring out this so-called truth and coming up with a plan to save everyone.

Jed was wearing his cowboy boots now, with shorts. Add in the cut on his cheek, and no wonder everyone they passed was giving him the oddest look, but right now Andy didn't care. They kept moving. This entire holiday had turned into a living nightmare that he wasn't ready to admit could end badly. One step at a time. One problem at a time. That was where they were at. That was where he had to keep his head.

"So you think there's any truth to what Xander heard about the land and Uncle Rodney?" Andy asked.

Jed scowled as they reached Neil's door, and he tapped on it. "Hell, no. This is my dad, not yours," he snapped.

Andy had the urge to tell Jed to fuck off. He could be an asshole when his back was against the wall, but Andy had seen the doubt there for just a second. Yeah, he just wasn't ready to admit his dad could have done something like that.

The door was opened by Jeremy, who was still in swim trunks and shirtless. His dark hair was a mess, and his gaze connected with Andy's for a second.

"So what have you dug up?" Jed said, already in the room as Andy stepped in.

He could hear voices, and he took a second with his son, resting his hand on his bare shoulder, suddenly feeling how young he was. "How're you holding up with all this?" he asked.

Jeremy just shook his head and blew out a frustrated breath. "Seriously, Dad? Never in my wildest dreams. I just want them to be okay, and then I'd be all right with all of us hopping on a plane and going home. Did Rodney really do something like that?"

He took in his son and dragged his gaze over to where Jed was standing and talking with Ric, Danny, and Xander. Mark was there, too, along with the head of security for the resort, a man named Edgar. Michael stepped out of one of the bedrooms, now barefoot and in a pair of navy shorts and a white T-shirt. He looked so much like Neil, Andy thought.

He turned back to Jeremy. "Honestly, I can't say for sure. I told you about my dad. If it had been him, then yeah, I'd guarantee it. Even his dad, my grandfather, who I never met but heard stories about, wasn't above using his means to get what he wanted—but never my uncle. However, I've learned sometimes we just can't know every-thing about someone's past." He patted Jeremy's cheek. He knew he hadn't really answered his question. They both stepped in.

The suite had the same layout as his, as Diana and Jed's. They were the top of the line, and there were only ten in the entire resort. Jed was already conferring with Edgar, and Steven appeared from the kitchen, this time with a bottle of water. Yeah, he was still on edge. Gabriel was shaking his head, his gaze reaching out to Andy from across the room. His expression mirrored the disbelief and shock Andy was feeling.

"Edgar says he has a friend in the department who can help," Jed said.

The way Edgar watched them all, Andy knew there was more. "Yes," the man said, "but we must be careful. There are four cartels in the area, smuggling, and they have deep ties to the Mexican police. There is a lot of corruption. It wouldn't serve us well in this situation, but at the same time, I hear from Xander that two are shot, and Neil and his father are also injured. In that case, I would suggest that bringing in the police may be the smarter choice. At least I can reach out to my friend and let him know the situation."

Andy wasn't sure what Xander was doing at the kitchen table. He was on a laptop, and Ric was leaning over his shoulder. He said something to him in a low voice before lifting his gaze to Andy and gesturing for his attention.

Andy realized Edgar was waiting for his approval, and for a second he realized that this could all land on his shoulders. Maybe he out of all of them could see this objectively. "Call him," he said. "Tell him the situation, but under no circumstances do they go in guns blazing."

Xander was typing and then leaned back in his chair, lifting his gaze. "I disagree, Edgar," he said. "Andy, sorry, but I was in the house. These are two Americans with nothing to lose. From what I heard, they weren't random thugs. This is a man who wants payback, and just call it a feeling, but I'm pretty damn sure Davis won't hesitate to shoot. The police could make him feel cornered, and we're not dealing with someone who wants to be reasoned with. Whatever he believes happened, it was a lifetime ago, yet he's carried it for all these years. That's not a man who's going to just give up and surrender. He'll go down fighting and take everyone with him, because he blames them, all of them, for his misery…" Xander hit enter on his computer and pulled up something on screen.

Ric stepped over to Andy and said in a low voice, "I just heard back from my brother, Morgan. He's managed to have our investigator do some digging. Apparently some forty years ago, there was a two-acre parcel of land surrounded by what is now Brad's ranch. Then it became part of the Friessen property. There were other land purchases, but that one stood out because the owner's name was Gary Davis."

Xander slid his laptop over.

Danny was right there, hands on the table, looking at it. "Shit," he said. "Gramps screwed someone?"

Chris swore behind him, and Andy crossed his arms over his chest and pulled in a breath, taking in the shock on everyone's faces. He did his best to get his head together.

"Just wait. Do we know how he came to have the land?" he said. "Did he buy it, something…?"

Xander had a way of looking at people that was both cocky and let them know he had something to say. "Can't say for sure. Doesn't say it was used to settle a debt or sold, just that one year it belonged to Davis, the next to your dad. I'd have to do more digging to find out, but do we really have that kind of time?"

There was a pounding on the door, and Jeremy opened it. It was Diana, with Emily, who looked like hell, blood on her shirt and her face a mess, her eyes swollen red from crying. Steven grabbed her and hugged her.

"Emily just got here," Diana said. "Tom took Becky to the hospital. Emily, tell them what you told us."

"How is Becky?" Jed called out. "Neil, Brad, my mom and dad…what happened?"

The questions were flying, and Andy could see Emily was going to lose it when Steven stepped back. She was wound so tight that the demands on her, the questions, were too much.

"Stop, all of you!" she yelled. "They're still there. Brad talked Davis into letting us go, saying he and Rodney would stay. Davis said no, that just Becky and Tom and me and Neil could go. Brad said Neil had to go to get him what he wanted, but he said he's going to shoot Brad! He's going to kill him, and Brad knows it! He was trying to save everyone, Neil too. God damn him!" Emily cried out. "He made Candy stay to keep Neil in line so he gets him what he wants, the ranch. He wants all of it, the land… He believes some land was stolen from his dad. This isn't a reasonable man. Becky and Rodney are still in there. He wouldn't let your mom go, your grandma." She took them all in. "He's crazy and angry—and Neil stayed behind. We got into the garage, drove here in Rodney's SUV. Neil broke into the gun locker. He has a rifle, I think, and…"

Diana slid her arm around Emily and held her close. Jed just lifted his gaze to Andy. Andy knew what he was thinking, and he heard a chair slide back. Xander was on his feet, walking to the door.

"Xander, where are you going?" Andy called out.

"Back to the estate," he said. "Jed told me that I got Neil when I married Cat. Yeah, he's a pain in the ass, but there's no way I'm letting him do what I think he's going to do. I love my wife, and she loves her dad, her mom, her family—so yeah, I kind of have to love them too. I'm going in there to save his ass."

"What about the truth you wanted to dig up?" Andy was trying to keep his head together, but Xander just stood for a second, letting his gaze linger on the group.

"We need to give him what he wants, the truth he wants to hear," he finally said. "Neil is trying to play cop, but he's better in the boardroom, and that's something that could get him killed along with everyone else. I won't be putting him in the ground."

Arrogant, confident. Andy dragged his gaze over to Jed.

"I think we had better tag along," he said.

Brad could hear his dad's raspy breathing and didn't know how much he could take. For the first time, his dad was starting to look like an old man. He could see Candy now that the chair Neil had been sitting in was empty. It gave him some peace, knowing that his wife and daughter and brother were safe.

Now Brad wouldn't have to sit there and watch as Davis put a gun to Neil's head and pulled the trigger. He wouldn't do that. He couldn't.

Candy must have known, as the love in her expression reached out to him. It wasn't that he'd given up, because he wouldn't, but at the same time, he'd seen the look in Davis's eyes. It was the look of a hardened man life had kicked in the head over and over, one who would go out shooting before ever giving in.

He wouldn't be reasoned with. Brad wondered at what point he'd been broken.

"Robbie, you said you landed in foster care and did time, as well. Where?"

Davis was over by the window, glancing out. Alan was

on the sofa, sitting, staring at him with a look that said he'd like them to hurry this along and shoot him, but thankfully, he'd said nothing more. He scratched his bare arm over and over.

"Why do you want to know?" Davis said as he walked over, dropping his gaze to Rodney, still on the floor, and then dragging that hateful look over to his mom. There was disdain there, the kind Brad had never seen before.

"You've been holding on to this for a lot of years. I guess I just want to know what happened to you. Did you marry, do you have kids?" There had to be something human in there. Brad could see a whole lot of hurt that had to be driving him.

"Well, let's see. After I aged out of foster care and hit the streets, I moved to the other side of the country, thinking it would make a difference to the hate I felt for your family, that the distance all those states over would help. Sure, I tried to do the life thing. Got a ton of jobs, met a girl, had a kid, joined the marines. Did a tour, came back, and she was gone, fucked off with my kid. I found her, and she'd hooked up with some loser. I settled the score, beat him to teach him you don't touch another man's woman, and pulled a gun on him. She was screaming the whole time, my kid in the next room crying. I left, just walked out, furious because she didn't even send a Dear John. It was just oops, gone, hooked up with some lowlife. Cops picked me up. Got a public defender, said I should plead out and I'd likely get three years' probation and get discharged from the marines. Yup, I fucked up and knew it, so I listened, but nope. Judge didn't take kindly to someone fresh out of the marines with a chip on his shoulder and angry at life, with a score to settle. Got charged with assault and intent, and he slapped me with the maximum, twenty years at Smith in Georgia. Gave me a lot of years to reflect on everything: my life, what you took from me, and how some just never get a break. Prison shrink said I had anger issues, but who the fuck doesn't?

"He said I needed to find a way to channel it positively, so I made it my life's mission to find out everything about all of you, the family that took from mine, and to see that Rodney got payback. In all the time I had, digging, I learned Rodney and his wife had a huge spread down on the Yucatan, with vast wealth and a resort for Neil. Jed married and was off on his own, and you, Brad, got the family ranch, a wife, a family, and you built an empire of more and more. All of you were living the dream, having it all and then some. You were a happy family who got to have a life, a happy life, with nothing yanked from under you. I mean, Rodney, who did you screw down here to get all this?"

Robbie gestured to the living room, but Brad knew what he meant. "It started with the piece my dad had," he said. "It was in your way. That was what you said when I sat there and listened to you. My dad's small piece was right in the middle and was cutting off your access to water, mineral rights, or what? I could never figure it out. Doesn't it always come down to the most ridiculous things? I remember you put some lien on the property, and my dad called you a liar. He never knew how you did it, but he packed everything up. It was just us, and we left, because my dad knew you would follow through on your threat and have him arrested on a bunch of trumped-up charges, including trespassing on land that was actually his. What kind of fucked-up world is this that a man can just take another man's land? Your dad was a senator, and you had that clout and power and money behind you."

Robbie snapped his fingers. Brad could see the toll this

was taking on his mom as he tried to picture the land, knowing it was still just that.

"Robbie, nothing was done with that land," Rodney said. "It's still there. It's just sitting there."

Saying that wouldn't help, and the look he got from Davis said just as much. "Well, that's even worse. You kicked my dad and me to the curb and stole just because you could. You really are a piece of shit, Rodney Friessen."

He caught motion out of his peripheral, and then there was a pop. Davis jerked, and he saw blood. It was Xander or Andy. They were there, and all hell broke loose.

Ric somehow managed to take down Alan, and he had the gun. Xander had Davis on the ground, his gun sliding across the floor, and he punched him in the face over and over. Then there was Jed, who was with him. They had the man pinned down. As Brad looked up, he couldn't believe it. There was Edgar from the resort, along with Danny, Chris, Mark, Steven, Jeremy, Michael, and Gabriel, all with guns, rifles, shotguns from his dad's locker.

Then Mark was untying his hands, saying, "It's going to be okay, Uncle Brad. It's over. We'll get you to the hospital."

"Are you okay?" said Steven, who was working on his legs. "You look like shit. God dammit, Brad. Don't do that again." Steven actually put his arms around him and brushed his shoulder, and he thought he'd go blind from the pain. He yelled, and Steven pulled back, but he could see how shook up he was.

"I'm fine," Brad said. "I can't believe this…"

He had to stop talking as he pulled his hands free from the rope that had confined them for so long. The pain shot through his arms, his shoulders—and then there was Neil, standing before him, a semiautomatic in his hand and a look in his eyes that he'd never seen before.

"You came back," Brad said.

Neil stumbled a bit, and Gabriel grabbed his arm and put his hand on the semiautomatic to take it from him.

"Whoa, there," Gabriel said. "You need to get to the hospital, too."

Candy was up and in his arms, and Michael too, his arms around his mom and dad. Brad spotted two Mexican police, who had Davis cuffed. He was bleeding on the floor, swearing, but he stopped fighting as he was pulled to his feet. Alan was already gone. Brad could see him cuffed, being walked out of the house. When he dragged his gaze back, Davis was staring at him and then Neil, and then his dad, who was untied and now being helped up by Jed and Danny.

"So you still win," Davis said, sounding so much like a man defeated. "You get everything, and you just get away with what you did." He was pulled roughly by one of the cops, and he yelled out in pain, blood running down his arm.

Someone had put a blanket around his mom and his dad. Brad could see how blood had dried around the side of Rodney's head, his ear, and he didn't know what to say.

"Mister Friessen, we'll get you all to the hospital," Edgar said, standing in front of his dad. "I've already spoken with my friend in the police. The two here will be charged for breaking in, for their crimes…"

Brad stopped listening as Steven and Mark helped him from the chair. He had to struggle because of the cramping in his legs, his arms, and from being shot. He felt as if all his strength had drained out of him. His leg would have buckled if he hadn't been leaning on Steven.

"Becky, how is she?" he said. "Emily? All the kids?"

He was being walked out of the house along with Rodney and Becky ahead of him. An ambulance was pulling in the front, lights flashing, and he glanced to his dad, who was still talking with Edgar. At the cop car, where Alan and Davis were in back, Xander and Andy talked with the cops. His mom was loaded into the back of the ambulance, wearing an oxygen mask.

"Tom took her to the hospital," Steven said. "She's in surgery. That's all I know. Emily made it back to the resort. She's scared, upset, but we're fine. Everyone's fine. We're going to be fine." The way Steven said it, Brad knew he was still in shock. They all were.

Neil was refusing to get in the ambulance, and Brad could see him arguing with Candy and Jed, whose face was a mess with dried blood. He was looking very much the outlaw despite his ridiculous getup of cowboy boots with shorts, digging into each step as he headed straight for him. He somehow took over for Mark, slipping his arm around Brad, holding him up.

"You look like shit," Jed said, and Brad couldn't answer for a minute.

"I can't believe you guys did that," he said, "that you came in and…got us out." Maybe it hadn't quite sunk in. Jed and Steven helped him to the ambulance, as there was no way he could walk by himself.

"We were just the backup," Jed said as they reached the ambulance and Neil, who was now sitting against the side. "Got here just in time, as Neil was inside and was planning on getting you out himself."

"Get in the damn ambulance, Neil," Candy snapped. "I swear to God, you listen to me, because I'm not messing around here. I will make you if I have to." She was so mad, and the medic was crouching behind him, looking at his head. Neil winced as he hit a sore spot.

"Looks like stitches and likely a concussion. You'll need to see a doctor," the medic said.

Brad allowed his gaze to drift over to Jed and then Neil. "We're all going to the hospital, Neil, so get in the fucking ambulance—and thanks to all of you for getting us out."

Then his dad was there, being helped into the ambulance. No one said anything else, and as Neil climbed into the ambulance and sat beside them, his dad rested a hand on his shoulder. Brad was helped in and laid on the stretcher, and he could see the steel of the roof and hear the door closing.

For the first time in his life, as he lay there in silence, he didn't know what to say.

Jed was sitting in one of the chairs in Brad's large hospital room, his cheek stitched, Diana beside him. Andy noticed she didn't let him go far. Neil was in the other chair, with four stitches to the back of his head. A scan had revealed that he had a mild concussion, so he needed rest and quiet, but after one night in the hospital, he'd been released. Candy was perched on the arm of the chair beside him, her arm around him, appearing pensive.

Brad was still in the hospital bed after surgery and debridement of the damaged tissue. As the surgeon had said, he was lucky there was no nerve damage. Emily was on the bed with him, his hand in hers. An IV was in one of his arms, and he was on a heavy dose of antibiotics.

Then there was Becky, who was in the other bed in the room after surgery to repair a damaged vein and remove the bullet. She'd been given two bags of transfused blood for her blood loss, but all in all, they'd been lucky. Even his uncle, who had a severe concussion and was still recovering from the ordeal, was doing remarkably well. Rodney was in a room down the hall with his aunt, who'd been kept overnight for observation as well. Because of the stress, her age, and the potential for another stroke, the doctors had been over-cautious.

Tom had been hovering close to Becky, not letting her out of his sight, fussing and checking her monitor, IV, and vitals even after the doctor said she was going to be fine. Of course, Tom had been keeping an eye on Rodney, the elder Becky, and Brad as well, and through this, Andy sensed both a sorrow and a bond between them, all of them, that he knew was unbreakable. They'd been close before, but now they'd survived something.

Laura slid her arm around his waist. Her blond hair was pulled up, and she was wearing an off-the-shoulder mixed blue sundress. Andy took in how quiet everyone was.

"So did Dad say why he wanted to talk to us?" Jed asked, but Brad wouldn't look his way.

Becky appeared sleepy and opened her eyes a minute before letting them fall closed again. Tom pressed the button for her bed and raised the head up, then leaned down and kissed her. She lifted her hand and touched his cheek. He was hovering and looked like he needed some sleep.

"No," Brad finally replied, "just that he wanted everyone here and all the grandkids. Said it couldn't wait."

Andy could see how uncomfortable Neil was, as well. He heard talking, and the door opened, and in stepped Steven and Katy with Jack and Fletcher. Xander followed, pushing a wheelchair that carried Rodney. Cat was carrying the baby, and she walked right over to Neil, who took his grandson. His aunt was dressed and walking with Chelsea, who was holding her arm. Ric was behind her along with Sara and Zac, Jeremy, Gabriel, Mark, Chris and

JD, Danny and Evie, and Michael, and the once spacious hospital room was suddenly overcrowded. Jack sat at the foot of Brad's bed, his hand on his dad's leg, and Fletcher was beside him.

"Where're Elizabeth and Tiffy?" Andy said to Gabriel, who leaned against the wall beside him.

"We thought having all the young ones here would be too much, so Angie, Elizabeth, and Tiffy volunteered to stay behind with them," Gabriel said. "Trevor and Jasmine, too. I'm thinking by the look of the room, all of us crowded in here, we don't need the kids running around. Besides, I got the impression that whatever Rodney wants to say, maybe they shouldn't be here."

The way Gabriel explained it, Andy knew his son understood that more was going on here than anyone else wanted to admit.

"Thanks for coming, everyone," Rodney said. Andy took in his uncle, who looked frail, a bandage on the side of his head. Xander had moved the wheelchair so Rodney was facing all of them, and Ric had pulled a chair over for the elder Becky, who was now sitting, not at all the happy aunt he remembered.

"This isn't the reunion we wanted for all of you here," Rodney said. "This was supposed to be a fun celebration to see all of you and how you've grown, to catch up. This family is getter bigger. My grandkids are grown and married and having kids of their own, and we don't get to see you all like we once did. You've all moved on with your lives, and it seems everyone is busy. I didn't believe I would get to have this moment with you, to see you again… It's humbling for a man to be on the ground with a gun to his head, knowing he's going to meet his maker, but worse than that, I feared my loved ones were going to suffer that fate as well because of a choice I made in what seems like another lifetime. I'm sure you're all wondering if there was any truth to Robbie Davis's allegations."

Andy already knew some of the story, and he found his gaze drifting over to Xander, who was standing behind Cat, his arms around her. They stood beside Neil, who was still holding his grandson.

"It's okay, Grandpa. You don't have to say anything," Jack said as he reached over and touched his grandfather's shoulder.

Rodney smiled and pressed his aged hand over Jack's, patting it. "Thanks, Jack, but this is something I have to say. You know being a man means owning up when you do something wrong."

Jack leaned back, and Rodney looked at all of them, especially his grandkids.

"The world breaks everyone," he started. "There's no shame in being a broken man, but you need to pick up the pieces and start rebuilding. The shame is giving up. This situation was about two acres of land, an old house built on a piece of property that had been won in a poker game."

Jed looked on in disbelief, while Neil smiled down at his grandson and didn't look his dad's way. Andy wondered if he'd already heard the rest.

"You won the property in a poker game?" Zac asked from where he stood in front of Laura. Andy rested his hand on the top of his son's head.

"No, Zac," Rodney replied. "Not me. My grandfather had bargained a piece of our property away on the tables at a backwoods game, and then Gary Davis eventually inherited it. It was on the east side of the property, and they had to always cut across our property to get to their house, right through where the cattle grazed. That would have worked fine if we neighbors got along, but

Gary and I were at odds more than not. One of the things I did was pay attention to my father. As senator, he had always said there was a way to get what you want. After digging, I found there had been no official record of a transfer of rights, a deed of sale. There was just a piece of paper that was easy enough to make go away after a call to the right people, a friend of my father's, the county clerk. Then the property was mine. It had been in our family since settlers had first come out that way."

Brad was still looking away, at no one but Emily, and both seemed resigned. Brad was the one who now had the land in question, all of it, and it clearly didn't sit right with him. No one said anything, and Rodney shifted his gaze over to the elder Becky.

"My wife didn't know everything…"

"That's not true, Rodney," she said. "I knew enough. I knew you'd done something, considering the way you and Gary always went at things. You hated the junk he'd leave lying around, the fences he took down, the fact that his house was right in that prime spot. You kept saying it was an eyesore, but it was more that you two would never be friends. He hated the cows, the herd, and scared them off with a shot now and again. You tried to reason with him, but I watched you throw up your hands and say one way or another, he had to go. So I knew something had happened. I just didn't ask, because there was suddenly peace."

Rodney nodded. "But it wasn't that simple. I was so full of myself, arrogant and happy that it was mine. When I showed up and served Gary the eviction papers, we argued, and I never paid any mind to the little boy, his son, who was there. I told him to pack up, gave him twenty-four hours, and then I'd have him charged with criminal trespassing and hauled out of there and thrown in jail." Rodney's hands rested on his lap.

"So you told him, Gramps, to leave and not ever come back? You took away their home?" Becky sounded so weak. Andy hadn't known she was awake. Tom was beside her, his arm around her head, her pillow.

"I was wrong to do what I did, and I knew it not long after, when I got word that Gary Davis had killed himself. I even tried to justify it, saying it hadn't really been his land. My grandfather had been a drunk fool, and who was to say if the bet was even legal? Perhaps he had been cheated out of his property. You start to justify what you do and come up with all kinds of reasons to excuse it, some lie to convince yourself that you were right. Well, I was wrong, and right now, I'm a man who's asking your forgiveness for what I did." He looked at all of them, and Andy didn't know how his uncle could sit there and humble himself before them. He'd never expected to hear this kind of confession.

"Well, of course we forgive you," Danny said. Chris nodded, and so did Sara, and while Andy could see everyone else nod, he wondered if they really did.

"Thanks for that, Danny, but if you can't forgive me and need time, I understand," Rodney said. "Just know I love all of you very much. You're my family, which is why I needed you kids to know what I did. I hope you can learn from me. You need to be able to look yourself in the mirror every day and know and believe that you've done the right thing, that you love yourself, that you haven't done anything you're not proud of. Learn from what I did. My dad was an accomplished man, a powerful man, and he got what he wanted by whatever means he deemed necessary. He was a United States senator, a man many looked up to, but his ideas of fair play were something I'm deeply embarrassed to have ever believed. That was no way for a man to behave. He was not a role model, and neither am I. Do better." He allowed his gaze to take in all of them. "No man, woman, or child has never done something they aren't deeply ashamed of, but that makes you human. What makes you decent is admitting what you did, saying you're sorry, and finding a way to make it right."

There was a hum of voices, and Laura slid her hand into his. He looked down at her. There was so much love there, and just listening to his uncle, Andy had thought of everything he'd done in the past that he wasn't proud of and never wanted to share with anyone. Maybe his uncle was the better man.

"Dad and I talked," Brad said, cutting in. "Emily and I have discussed this at length, and we're selling the ranch, all of it."

Andy wasn't sure who was more surprised—the kids, Neil, or Jed. The way Steven and Katy looked at each other, he knew this was the first they were hearing it.

"Why?" Neil said. "Brad, you love the ranch, and how can you even sell it? I thought Granddad's covenant on the property made sure it would always be passed down to the eldest son."

Rodney actually chuckled, lifted his hand to his head, and shook it gently. "Well, my father was a fool, arrogant. It's time this was made right. A lawyer will get the covenant overturned, and Robbie will be given what's rightfully his."

Andy wasn't sure what to say, but Jed was fuming.

"You're excusing what he did?" he snapped. "He was going to kill you, and Brad, and Neil, and even Becky! How can you even say that?" Jed was loud when he was pissed, and Neil and Brad exchanged a glance.

"No," Rodney said. "I'm not excusing what he did. He

terrorized us, and I'm furious that you all got dragged into something that was of my making—but maybe I had a hand in making him into what he is. If I hadn't done what I did, he wouldn't have had the life he did."

"You don't know that, Dad," Neil said.

"You're right, I don't, but I do know the minute his dad killed himself over something I did, I set in motion a life for him that I wouldn't want for my worst enemy."

Andy lifted his hand. "You know what? I hear all of you, and I appreciate what you're willing to do, Uncle Rodney, but at the same time, Robbie had a choice. I'm not a saint, never said I was, and if we all start comparing things we've done in our pasts, I'm sure our kids would likely wonder how they turned out as well as they did. You had some responsibility there, but so did Robbie. As an adult now, he's responsible for his choices. Just because he's screwed up, you can't say it's not his fault. He doesn't get a pass."

"No one is saying he does, Andy," Brad cut in, "but he gets an apology and something that should have been his."

"You mean the ranch?" Jed said. Diana slid her hand over his shoulder, but as she did so, she lifted her gaze over to Andy. There would always be that thing between them, even though they were family now.

"No, I'm selling the ranch," Brad said. "He'll get his part. That's it, no more, no less."

"Dad, you can't sell the ranch," Jack said. "What about the horses, the cattle? Where will we take them?"

Fletcher and Katy, too, seemed a little torn.

"Hey, I don't know," Brad said. "We'll get another place. But it's time, anyways, that I got out of the cattle business. The ranch has been my life, our life, and I love that place, but you know what? Someone else will love it and work it, and we're going to be fine somewhere else. A fresh start doesn't hurt anyone, and it doesn't matter where we are—we have each other. We'll figure it out, okay?"

"So what happens to Robbie Davis, then?" Becky said. "And the guy with him? Dad, he's a bad person, and you're just going to pay him? I hope they both rot in jail and they never let them out. I'm sorry, but I can't be as forgiving."

That was a bitter pill, and Andy couldn't blame Becky for feeling that way.

"Well, what I did to his father was worse," Rodney said, turning in his chair to face her. "Can you forgive me for that?"

Andy took in the surprise, the shock on her face as she replied, "Well, of course, but you're not a bad man. I saw his face, the way he hated me, and I did nothing to him." She was kind of right.

"You won't see him again," Rodney said. "It's up to you, but remember the only one you're hurting by not forgiving him is yourself. What he did was because of his hate for me. He wasn't able to forgive and move on."

That had Becky thinking, considering. At the same time, Andy knew she wasn't there yet. Could he blame her, after what she'd been through? No.

"Okay, I'm kind of tired," Rodney said, "and my age is catching up to me. Michael, take me back to my room. I think the rest of you should try to enjoy yourselves at the resort, and take your grandma back with you."

Andy watched as Michael wheeled Rodney out, and shortly after, he and Laura stepped out of the room and waited for the kids to follow.

"Hey, I'm going to ride with everyone back to the resort," Laura said. "Are you coming?"

"No, I'm going to hang back a second. I'll see you back there." He leaned down and kissed Laura and then, after saying goodbye to Brad and Becky and Emily and Tom, who had no intention of leaving, moved back into the hallway along with the rest of the family. As the crew made their way to the elevators at the end of the hall, Andy hung back with Xander. It was chaos, and he needed a minute.

"So what ended up happening to Robbie Davis?" he said.

"Rodney got him out of the hospital jail," Xander said. "Told the police it was a misunderstanding. They met this morning, and I was there when Rodney told him the truth and paid him."

Andy didn't know what to say. "And you think that will be enough?"

Xander just shrugged. "I don't know, but at least it's out in the open. He wanted the truth, an apology, and compensation. Won't bring his dad back, or his life, but at least Rodney gave him the chance for a new start. It's his choice what he does with it."

"You think he'll leave everyone be and not come back for more? Do Brad, Jed, and Neil know?" He didn't know how everyone would react.

Xander pulled in a breath and crossed his arms. "Brad knows. Jed, Becky, Emily, and Candy? No, they wouldn't understand. Neil…I'll tell him. Honestly, it seemed Davis didn't expect this from Rodney. They'll never be friends, but time will tell," Xander said.

"And the other guy…?" Andy couldn't remember his name.

"Alan was just along for the ride, just someone Davis did time with. He's an addict. I'll give him two months, tops, but he'll find his own way back to prison."

Andy took in Ric, who was walking back their way. "Come on, you two. We're grabbing some beers back at the resort. Neil's put a call in, and they're setting up dinner for us on the balcony of his penthouse—our own private party." Ric's gaze lingered between Andy and Xander. "We good here?"

Andy just wiped his jaw. "He knows, doesn't he?" he asked Xander.

Xander shrugged. "It was Ric's idea to let him go, and he's right: Everything isn't always black and white."

Andy shook his head and started walking toward the elevator. Some of his family had already left, while others had taken the stairs.

"Oh, and one other thing," Xander said, catching up to him and pressing his hand to his arm. "Don't tell Neil what I said about having to love him. That's just one of those things that can be left unsaid."

Andy couldn't fight the urge to smile. "Yeah, he would hold it over your head forever."

"So beer, dinner, and catching up with everyone? Not the reunion I was expecting," Ric said as he jabbed the elevator button.

"Nope," Andy said, "but everyone's alive, and you know what? Family really is everything."

"You've been really quiet, sitting over here all by yourself," Xander said as he scraped back a metal patio chair on the expansive balcony of the penthouse suite and sat down beside Neil. Candy, Emily, Laura, and Diana were in the hot tub, and he took in the rest of the family talking, laughing, and the long table of food. One of the chefs was carving a piece of meat for Mark, what Neil thought was his third plateful.

"Just taking everything in," Neil said. He found himself counting everyone. Would the horror of what they'd lived through four days earlier ever allow him to feel that peace and security he'd felt with his family again? He doubted it.

"You've been doing a lot of that lately, being less of a pain in the ass," Xander said.

Neil leaned back and rested his beer on the table. Xander was his daughter's husband, his grandson's father, a man he never would've picked for Cat. Now, he was still unable to say what he meant to him, considering he'd basically saved his ass and his family's. There wasn't a better man out there. He took in the way Xander was watching him, and for the first time, he realized he felt as if he didn't have to worry as much. There was just something about knowing someone had his back.

"I know you're going to take great pleasure in this, so I'm just going to say it," Neil said. "Thank you—for…" For finding him just as he'd come up the back stairs to the wine room off the dining room, dizzy and his head killing him as he tried to pull it together. Xander had grabbed his arm, held him up, and said nothing. "You saved my family, and I'm not too proud to admit that I wouldn't have been able to make the shot you did, wounding Robbie in the shoulder and making him drop the gun. You brought in the cavalry. I guess I never asked how you knew about the back way. I did because I was part of the build, and I had the drawings done up."

Xander watched him before dragging his gaze over to Cat, who was talking with Michael and Angie. A baby monitor, he could see, was clipped to the waistband of Xander's Bermuda shorts. "You forget what I do," Xander replied. "I make a point of knowing all the ins and outs of places. The estate, I figured that out long ago." He lifted his beer and took a swallow, his heavy gaze lingering a bit.

"Smart," Neil said. Brilliant, really. He hadn't expected that. "I guess what I'm trying to say is thank you for saving my wife, my brother, my parents…and me."

"I bet it was difficult for you to choke that out," Xander said. At any other time, the comment would have likely slipped under his skin, but Neil couldn't keep off the twitch of a smile that touched his lips.

"No," he said, noting the seriousness that came over Xander. He had to know how he felt about him. "We're a lot alike, Xander, but at times I wonder if you're the better man."

Xander froze with his beer lifted, about to take a drink.

He could see he hadn't expected that. Hell, Neil had never expected to say it. He cleared his throat roughly.

Across the patio, Brad, his arm in a sling, stopped at the hot tub, said something to Emily, and leaned in and kissed her. He smiled at all of the ladies, and whatever he said to them had Diana splashing him. He stepped back, laughing, before making his way over to Neil and Xander and pulling out one of the patio chairs beside them, where he sat down with a groan. Neil knew his brother was only a day out of the hospital, still recovering, still hurting, and he wondered how long the tightness in his chest would continue every time he saw his brother, knowing the choice he'd made to save everyone but himself, even though he told himself it was what he'd have done.

"You should take it easy there, Brad," he said.

Brad tossed a scowl his way. "Stop mothering me. I'm fine," he said and actually reached over to rest his hand on Neil's shoulder. He pulled it away as they took in Becky, who hobbled on crutches over to a lounge chair, Tom hovering before he sat at the foot of the lounger and rested a blanket over her legs. It was like watching two newlyweds, the closeness.

"How's she doing?" Neil gestured with his chin. He didn't have to say who he meant, as of course Brad knew they were all worried.

"Scared, sore, but she's going to be fine."

Neil reached over and pressed his hand to Brad's good arm. "I see that she and Tom seem to be good."

Brad took them in, and his gaze lingered. He seemed to be searching out Steven, Fletcher, Jack, Trevor, Jasmine, and Katy, who was carrying Gilly. "Yeah, nothing like a close call with death to bring perspective. Whatever differences they had aren't there now. He doesn't let her out of his sight. He hovers and checks on all of us."

Jed and Andy walked over with Rodney. The side of his head was still bruised around the stitches he'd received, and he seemed to be walking slower.

"Here, sit down, Dad," Jed said and pulled out a chair. Rodney sat beside Brad, and Jed pulled over another chair and sat down as well. Andy took a chair beside Xander. While Jed and Andy were in swim trunks and bare feet, with T-shirts, Rodney was in a yellow golf shirt and khaki shorts. He was still unusually pensive, and for a minute no one said anything.

"So," Jed began, breaking the silence, "I had a sit-down with Chris and Danny about building on the land I gave them. Needed to try to figure out where their heads were, as Danny, Evie, and Sophie are still living in the loft above the barn, and Chris, JD, and Ally are in the house with us, and both seem comfortable with the status quo. Mark hasn't figured out where his head is. He's almost done school and hasn't given Diana or me any idea of his interests." He glanced over to his boys, who were looking over the balcony, talking. JD and Evie were with Elizabeth and Tiffy on the lounge chairs at the far end of the balcony, sharing what looked like a pitcher of margaritas.

"And?" Neil found this part of Jed irritating, where he kind of just left people hanging.

"And nothing," he replied. "Mark just did the Mark thing, said he'd think about it. Danny said he'll get on it after his big case that's coming up, and Chris said he'll talk to JD to see what she wants to build. Other than that, nowhere."

Neil just shook his head. These simple things really weren't a problem. "Does it matter?" he said. "At least they're there."

Jed just lifted his gaze and allowed it to connect with him as if he was trying to get into his head. "And what about you, brother? You've been pretty quiet the last few days. It's not like you not to have an opinion about everything."

Even his dad looked over to him, and he could see the question there.

"Just needed some time to figure this out," Neil said. "I'm still not sure I'm okay with you letting Robbie Davis walk." He looked over to Brad, who was staring down at the table, and he could tell he was thinking some pretty dark thoughts. "And you, deciding to sell the ranch? You love that place, always have."

Brad flicked his gaze over to him and then took in each of them. "I love my family more. It's not the same now. It's just land, which can't replace my family, so yeah, Neil, I'm good with it. I think it's time the Friessen legacy ended there and I start a new chapter for my family, kind of like Andy did," Brad added as he settled his gaze on his cousin.

Andy lifted a brow and reclined in his chair. "You planning on moving to Montana? Would love to have you," he said.

This time Brad did smile. "No, Montana is all yours. We'll find something in the area or up the peninsula, something that will work for all of us. Tom and Becky are still in Hoquiam, and Emily will never agree to go too far. Then there's you." Brad lifted his hand and slapped Neil's chest, trying to lighten the mood, but Neil knew what he was saying. He wasn't about to move away from him, either.

"Well, we kind of have an announcement, too," Rodney said and pulled in a breath. "Your mother and I are getting on in age, and this thing that happened with Robbie, I know you're all not okay with how I handled it, getting him released. Maybe I was wrong, but I did owe him. I can't turn back the clock and undo what I did, but if I want him to forgive me, then I suppose it had to start with me. He was released from the hospital yesterday, and I gave him a ticket back to Georgia. He has a daughter he's going to try to reconnect with, and he has enough money now to buy something for himself." His dad crossed his arms over his chest. "And your mother and I are putting the estate up for sale, selling all of it, the land, the cattle, everything. After what happened, we can't go back there, not at our age. You know, having Robbie show up at the door and your mother answering it only to have a gun in her face, being terrorized because someone hated me so much, it gave us a lot to consider. Being down here and away from you kids, our grandkids, isn't something we want anymore."

Even Andy seemed surprised.

"You sure, Dad? Where're you going to go?" Jed asked.

Rodney let his gaze linger on Neil, maybe because he was the only one who hadn't said anything to him since he'd learned what he'd done. Since his confession.

"Well, if you boys are okay with it, your mother and I would like to move up closer to you."

Neil said nothing at first, knowing his dad was waiting. Finally, he said, "I think that would be nice, Dad," and he allowed his gaze to drift over to Xander, who he knew could tell what he was thinking more than anyone, now.

Candy, Laura, Emily, and Diana strode over, dripping, towels wrapped around them. Candy sat on his knee, and he took in both Diana, Laura, and Emily doing the same with their husbands, although Emily was careful not to hurt Brad's shoulder.

"You're getting me all wet," Neil said, and Candy just wrapped her arm around him more. He could hear the laughter that picked up around the table.

"You'll dry," she teased.

"So what were you all talking about over here, looking so serious?" Diana said as Jed set his arm around her.

"Oh, just family," Brad said.

"And what's really important," Neil added, then took in his dad and allowed his gaze to soften. Yeah, he understood.

Rodney's eyes had suddenly turned misty. "Well, if you'll excuse me, I think I'll go find your mother. I'm getting tired, so we're going to turn in to that nice comfortable room you put us up in, Neil." His dad stood up and then took them in, each of them. "I may not have said this enough, but I love all of you very much." Then he walked away over to his wife, their mother, who was sitting and talking with Becky and Tom.

"You think your dad's going to be okay?" Emily asked.

Neil could feel the way Candy tightened her arm around him. He ran his hand up her bare thigh to her swimsuit bottoms.

In the chair beside him, Xander finished the rest of his beer, rested the bottle on the table, and slid his chair back. "Well, I'm going to leave you kids and go find my own wife," he said.

Neil touched his arm. "Hey, I meant what I said."

Xander just held his gaze for a second and then nodded. "I know: I'm your favorite son-in-law."

Everyone started laughing.

When They Were Young

A FRIESSEN FAMILY SHORT STORY

Chapter 1

This would all be his one day.

Being the eldest of three boys, twelve-year-old Brad Friessen knew that this cattle ranch outside Hoquiam, Washington, which encompassed three hundred acres bordering the state park and had been in the family since the first Friessen settled in the Pacific Northwest in the late 1800s—1859, to be exact—would all be his to run, to own, to have. Over the last few years, his father had aggressively bought up the surrounding land and property before developers could get their hands on it, amassing another hundred acres. Brad made a point of listening when his mom and dad were talking. His dad was a brilliant man, and Brad believed he would soon own everything on this side of the peninsula. It made him feel proud to have that kind of power behind him.

It was a history few families had, but as his father, Rodney Friessen, had told him many times, the Friessen name meant something here. Brad's grandfather, Angus Friessen, had been a state senator and president of the Cattlemen's Association. Although Brad had never met him, considering he'd died before he was born, he had heard stories about how he could make anything happen. Angus Friessen had been a powerful man. This was his part of the country.

"Brad," his dad called out to him, stepping out the back door of the house, his blue jeans tucked into gumboots. He was tall, strong, dark haired, and the kind of man Brad wanted to be.

Brad held the reins of his quarter horse, Bucky, already saddled, and took in his dad heading his way.

"Where're you off to?" Rodney said. "I thought I told you to clean out all the stalls in the barn."

Of course he had, and Brad had done just that. He was about to reply when he heard the clomping of another horse and turned to see Neil coming out of the barn, leading his nearly all-black Arabian. Neil was a little shorter than Brad, but he had the same dark hair and amber eyes, and they'd always been unbelievably close.

"We did. I helped Brad," Neil said, stopping beside him, holding the reins. His horse had an attitude, and depending on the day, the season, or his general mood, he had thrown Neil a time or two. Brad suspected the horse was really a mirror to who Neil was at times, the brother who stood out and had to take center stage. "We've got things to do, Dad," Neil continued. "We're taking a ride out to our treehouse down at the ravine. We need to finish the roof. Robbie's probably already there. Come on, Dad, we can't keep him waiting. We're late now."

Brad wasn't sure what to make of his dad's expression, the way he took in Neil and then him. His face hinted he could say no just as easy as yes—just a feeling he had. "Dad, I've done everything you've said to do…" he started.

"Actually, you had your brother help you. That's different than doing it yourself. Neil, you were supposed to herd up all the horses, bring them in, brush them all down, and clean out their hooves. I'm pretty sure you didn't get to that," Rodney said without even a smile.

"You said over the weekend, Dad," Brad said. "It's only Saturday. I'll help Neil with the horses tomorrow." He was careful not to challenge his dad too much, which he'd done on more than one occasion, as his mom had pointed out. They were too much alike in too many ways.

"So you're meeting Robbie Davis," Rodney said.

Of course they were. They hung out all the time. They were friends. Brad just looked at his dad, seeing the way he seemed suddenly angry about something.

"Not sure I want you to hang out with him all the time," Rodney said. "It seems he's the only one you're ever with. And that's one of the things I wanted to talk to you about…"

"Dad, Robbie is my best friend," Neil said, cutting in. "You're not going to tell me I can't see him?"

Brad wasn't sure what to make of his dad, who pulled in a breath and settled his gaze on Neil.

"I'm just saying that I don't want you going over to Robbie's, not right now. I've got some business with his dad, so I want you to just steer clear for a bit." His dad took him in next as if letting him know it was up to him to get Neil to listen.

"Fine, can we go?" Brad said without elaborating on the fact that Robbie was going to be waiting for them. His dad gave him that heavy gaze and then nodded.

"And what about your brother?"

He knew his dad meant Jed, the baby, who was eight and always dogging his heels. "Dad, it's just me and Neil. We don't want Jed tagging along. We want to move fast." He didn't want to have to look after his brother, but he knew that was what his dad was going to say next.

"Too bad. Take Jed with you and look after him, or you don't go."

Brad was about to argue when Neil nudged him and said, "Sure, Jed can come if he wants to, but I'm pretty sure he didn't want to hang out with us today. Considering the roof we still need to put on the treehouse, I don't think Jed's going to be too interested in helping."

There he went. Neil could talk his way, or rather their way, out of anything, and it always sounded damn frickin' convincing. Brad had to fight the urge to laugh, considering he'd basically told Jed to get lost just that morning, though not in those words. He'd even dropped the "F" bomb, knowing his mom would likely give him an earful if she heard, but Brad had been brushing his teeth after breakfast, and his brother had wanted to hang out with him.

Brad had expected Jed to go tell their mom, who would, he knew, make him include him. That was what she always did, thinking that all of them had to hang around together all the time, being brothers. And then there was Brad's mouth, as if swearing wasn't something he'd heard his mom and dad both do. The fact was that Jed was so much younger that hanging out together felt like looking after him. Instead, he wanted to move fast and not have to worry about Jed giving his mom a blow by blow of everything they weren't supposed to be doing.

His dad gave an odd laugh under his breath as he stared down at Neil. The terseness of his lips had the hair on the back of Brad's neck standing up.

"Jed…" Rodney called out, and they didn't have to wait more than a second for the screen of the back door to squeak open.

"Yeah, Dad?" he answered, and Brad could feel his afternoon with just Neil and Robbie, hanging around with the freedom to do things he didn't want his parents knowing about, slipping away. Namely, they had planned to check on the cougar den they'd found under a huge uprooted tree, but Jed would definitely tell their mom, who would tell their dad, and Brad would likely be grounded for the next month. He just loved the challenge, the danger. It was what drove him and excited him.

"Your brothers are going out to the treehouse down at the ravine," Rodney said. "You know the one you helped build? They said you weren't interested in tagging along. Is that true?"

Jed stepped out of the house in his old cowboy boots, pulling at his jean jacket, his hair a lighter brown than his and Neil's and a scowl on his face as he strode their way. "If they're going to the treehouse, so am I. They didn't invite me," he added.

Brad was about ready to kick his brother, but the way his dad was staring down at him, he knew he'd figured out what he and Neil had been up to.

"I suggest you two give your brother a hand saddling up his horse," Rodney said, "and stay away from that cougar den. I know you, Brad and Neil. You two are always poking into trouble, not thinking it can hurt you. But hear me well: That mother cougar will go after Jed first, the smallest, so you make sure he sticks close."

Then his dad was walking into the barn and saying something to Jed, whom he could hear already opening the stall door of his paint, Trudy.

"Well, it could be worse," Neil said as he tied the lead rope of his mare to the ring on the side of the barn.

"Oh, and how is that? Because as I see it, having Jed tag along means we won't be having the fun we want to have today."

Neil just shrugged. "It'll be fine. Jed won't bother us.

He just wants to hang around. We'll make him do all the hard stuff. He's smaller than us and can get up into those tight places." Neil had a wicked side at times, but at the same time, he didn't have the same responsibility on his shoulders as Brad did. He wondered if his brother would ever understand what it was like to be the eldest.

Chapter 2

"Hey, it's about time you got here," Robbie called out from the platform, which was about five feet off the ground, built from branches and old pieces of wood they had dragged out that way. The ladder was a rusty metal one that he and Neil had taken from the pile of old farm equipment over by one of the sheds that stored the winter hay. Neil had said their dad would never miss it. Robbie wondered, though, considering he'd heard his dad talk about the problems he was having with Mr. Friessen. His dad had called him an asshole, so of course he was curious.

He watched as Brad, Neil, and Jed rode up on their horses and tied them in the little clearing they'd made below the treehouse.

Robbie squatted down in his bare feet. His shoes and socks were soaked from the walk over. He and his dad's small house was on the east side of the Friessen land, and they had always lived there. Neil, Brad, and Jed had always been his friends—well, mainly Neil, since they were the same age and in the same classes, and he thought they shared the same dreams. He was his bestie.

Brad was arrogant at times and loved telling them both what to do, and little Jed was a pissant with a mouth on him, not scared to tell his older brothers where to go. Just last week he'd flipped Brad the bird after dragging a huge branch that had to have weighed three times more than him to the fort and helping get it up the ladder. Robbie had no idea where a kid that size summoned the strength. His contribution had become the main part of the floor, and afterward Brad had told him to get lost. At the same time, he idolized Brad. Robbie knew that Brad didn't have a clue.

"Looks like you're almost done," Brad called out to him. Neil was already climbing up the ladder, carrying a small backpack he'd untied from the back of the horse, Jed behind him.

"Well, I waited hours for you guys. You were supposed to be here after breakfast. Got tired of waiting, so I managed to slide up the rest of the branches for the roof myself. Just need to do the one side and then we're done."

He could hear Brad on the ladder as Neil dumped the backpack on the floor and Jed crawled in on his knees and sat down.

"I brought snacks," Neil said. Jed sat beside him, waiting patiently.

"That's good, because I'm starving," Robbie said. Since his dad had left for work early that morning, he'd downed a bowl of Cheerios and then started walking. His dad was supposed to pick up groceries on the way home when he got off at the lumber yard. Otherwise, Robbie would've packed a sandwich, but the bread was gone, and all that was left were frozen hamburgers, canned peas and corn, a bag of potatoes, and cereal. Yeah, he'd finished the last of the milk, too.

He took in the bag of Doritos, a block of cheese, three apples, and a bag of chocolate chip cookies that Neil pulled out before handing him a can of cola. "Oh, nice," Robbie said as he popped the can. "Can always count on you, Neil."

Brad climbed onto their makeshift floor, feeling the creak. They'd never tested the weight with all of them up there, and Brad squatted down as if overseeing all of it before taking a look out and down to the horses.

"This is a great view. We did a great job. Maybe next weekend we can bring our sleeping bags and sleep up here for a night," Brad said.

"That would be so much fun," Jed called out, ripping open the bag of Doritos. He shoved his hand inside and stuffed a handful in his mouth.

"You're not coming, Jed," Brad said. "You're too young and little, and I'm not looking after you overnight. Besides, this isn't big enough for all of us to sleep up here, and this is our treehouse, not yours."

Oh, here we go. The Jed and Brad thing was about to start up again.

"I don't take up much room, and I'm not too little— and I helped build this, so it's as much mine as it is yours. Besides, Dad will say no. You're not sleeping out here, either."

Damn, Jed was smart. Robbie had to give him that. "Jed, you're right," he said. "It is all of ours, and we couldn't have built it without you. Brad, stop arguing with Jed. If it wasn't for him, we wouldn't be almost done."

Brad was evidently ready to argue some more. It wasn't lost on Robbie how he was always trying to take charge, tell them all what to do. "I'm the one who found the spot, and this is all going to be my land," he said.

Neil gave him a look that said he'd crossed a line. "Maybe so, Brad, but this treehouse is a shared project. It's all ours and will never be just yours. And, just for the record, this property isn't yours yet, and it'll be a lot of years before it is." Neil sat cross legged, reaching his hand in the backpack again. "You don't get to tell any of us who can come and who can't."

Neil did have a way of putting Brad in his place, Robbie thought. He expected Brad to start arguing.

"Jed, if we sleep up here, yeah, you can come too," Robbie said, knowing that would really piss off Brad. He could see the way Brad firmed his lips, ready to argue. Yeah, Robbie had gotten on his bad side a time or two.

"Cut it out, Brad," Neil said. He had pulled out a cutting board and a small sharp paring knife. "Let's just sit down, enjoy the snacks I brought, and stop bickering—because you both know Mom will likely be the one to say no, not Dad. I for one don't want to spend the few hours I get to spend out here arguing. You're not the boss."

"Neil, is that Mom's good knife?" Brad said as he reached for a ginger ale and popped the top, then sat down, crossing his legs and taking in Robbie's wet shoes and socks.

"I suppose. She won't miss it, though," Neil said as he sliced through the block of cheddar and then turned to Jed, who was watching him, and pointed to him with the knife. "And don't you go telling her."

Jed just nodded, looked over to Robbie, and smiled. Then he opened the bag of cookies and held it out, offering one first to Brad, who took it, and then Robbie.

"So what's going on with your dad?" Brad said as Robbie took a bite of his cookie and chewed. He could see the way Neil looked up. There was something going on, something he didn't know.

"Brad, I don't think we should be talking about this," Neil said.

Brad shrugged. "Why not? I'm kind of curious why Dad said what he did, making it sound as if he's got a problem with your dad. He actually told us to stay away, so I'm kind of wondering if you know what's going on."

Robbie lifted the cola and took a swallow, then looked over to Neil for a clue. Neil only shrugged, so Robbie said, "I don't think it's my dad. I'm pretty sure it's yours. I know mine called yours an asshole, and I heard him say that your dad thinks he can do whatever he wants, whenever he wants, and he was having none of that."

Actually, his dad had said Rodney Friessen was an entitled asshole who took from anyone and everyone. He had more than his fair share and should spread the wealth around, but he was just a greedy bastard. He'd thought that was just his dad blowing off steam, as he'd said the same about his boss at the lumber yard and the lady at the bank. Everyone, as far as he was concerned, was a crook.

"My dad wouldn't be the bad guy here," Brad said. "I'm sure your dad did something."

Robbie could feel the anger start right in the pit of his stomach as he looked over to Brad. He wanted to hit him.

"Hey, how about you both knock it off?" Neil said. "Let's stop talking about our dads. This is supposed to fun."

Jed was frowning as if he was considering what Brad had said.

"Sure," Robbie said, "but just the same, my dad isn't the kind of man who's going to let your dad get away with anything or push him around." He didn't know why he'd said that, mainly to have the last word and wipe that smug look off Brad's face. Brad thought he was the king of the castle or, in this case, the land.

"Robbie, seriously," Neil snapped.

He took in his friend, whom he'd shared just about everything with, and saw that he'd said too much. "Fine, truce. How about we all agree to not talk about our dads?"

Brad seemed a little too pissed, though. Jed said nothing as he looked from Brad to Neil and then over to him.

Neil finally held up the cutting board, offering Robbie the cut pieces of cheese, and said, "Yeah, no dad talk—and no one tells Mom I also took the block of cheese she just bought."

Chapter 3

"Go and make sure the coast is clear, Jed, so I can put the cutting board and knife back before Mom sees," Neil said after unsaddling his horse, brushing her down, and putting her in one of the stalls with a fleck of hay. Brad was already walking with his and Jed's horses to the paddock outside, where his dad's other six horses were grazing.

"Okay, that was so much fun. Are we going to go again tomorrow?" Jed said, walking beside him.

Neil leaned down and picked up his backpack from where he had rested it against the barn. "We'll try. Have to finish the horses first, so if you give me a hand, then we have a better chance of going. Dad said I had to get all the horses groomed this weekend."

"Yup, I'll help," Jed said before running toward the house and pulling open the screen door. Neil could hear him talking to someone—his dad, he thought, who stepped out of the house and down the steps, walking his way.

"You were gone a while. Any problems out there?" Rodney called out.

Jed peeked out the back door and held up his little hand for Neil to stop. Evidently, the coast wasn't clear.

"No, it was fun. Kind of lost track of time," Neil said. Behind him, he could hear Brad walking through the barn, his boots scraping the concrete.

"So you were hanging out with Robbie." His dad stared down at him with that look that said they were in a bit of trouble.

"Jed told you," Neil said. He hadn't meant to say it, but he could tell by the way his dad lifted his brows and didn't answer that it had been his brother, who clearly hadn't understood the instructions "Don't tell Dad we were with Robbie."

"Robbie is my friend, Dad. If you're having problems with his dad, then that's between you and him. I told Robbie the same thing." Neil squeezed the strap of his backpack, feeling his heart hammering, knowing that it wasn't smart to talk to his dad the way he did.

"If I tell you to stay away from someone, you will listen," Rodney said. "My issues with his father have nothing to do with Robbie, but I'm not comfortable with you hanging out with him, considering his father has become a sizeable problem for me."

Brad stopped beside him, and Neil wasn't sure what to make of what his dad was saying. He didn't know Gary Davis well, having only said hey and bye and answered a few questions about school now and then, things like did he like it and was he doing well, as well as the occasional warning not to go getting into trouble. That was it.

Rodney dragged his gaze over to Brad and let it linger. "And you, being the oldest, when I tell you to do something, you listen. When I trust that you'll listen and do as you're told, then you get to go off on your horse alone with your brothers. If not, you can hang out here and do a considerable amount of work, mucking out stalls, hosing down the barn, fixing fences, and digging in the mud, so much so that you'll have absolutely no free time other than for school and homework." The way he said it, Neil could feel the trouble they were in, but at the same time, it was Brad who was getting it. Neil always, for some reason, escaped his brother's fate.

"Okay, I get it, Dad," Brad said. "It won't happen again. Look, I don't know what's going on with you and Robbie's dad, but I do know that Robbie said his dad wasn't going to let you push him around."

Neil dragged his gaze up to Brad, surprised he'd repeated what Robbie said. Neil was still kind of pissed at the back and forth between Brad and Robbie about their dads. Today was supposed to have been fun, not a pissing match over whose dad was a better man. At the same time, he was bothered that Robbie's dad could pose a possible problem.

"Robbie said that?" Rodney asked. Neil just stared at Brad as he nodded.

"He said his dad called you an asshole, said you thought you could do whatever you wanted whenever you wanted, and he was having none of that. I don't know what's going on, Dad, but it sounds like Mr. Davis is pretty mad at you."

Neil wasn't sure what to say as Rodney rested his hand on Brad's shoulder and squeezed. He seemed to be thinking some pretty dark thoughts.

"You boys get the horses put away," he finally said. There it was, a change of subject.

"Mine's in the stall inside, and Brad put his and Jed's out to graze," Neil said, still squeezing the strap of the backpack.

His dad took in him and then Brad. "Well, you two,

don't worry about this thing with Robbie's dad. It will be rectified soon. Your mother has dinner almost ready. Go in and wash up."

Then his dad was gone, and Neil took in Jed, who was still at the back door and was now motioning to hurry up. The coast was clear.

"So why did you tell Dad what Robby said?" he asked Brad as they walked to the door.

Brad simply shoved his hands in his pockets and shrugged. "He's our dad. He should know."

Neil took in Brad, the way he looked past him to the barn and the house.

"You know what Dad always says," Brad continued. "Look after family first." Then he stepped into the house.

At the door, Jed whispered, "I'm sorry. It just slipped out. I didn't mean to tell Dad we were with Robbie."

What could Neil say? He had two brothers who couldn't keep their mouths shut. One was too little to understand the concept of not telling their mom and dad, and the other at times surprised him with what he chose to share.

Chapter 4

"Okay, the store was closed by the time I got there, so I picked us up a pizza," Robbie's dad said as he came in the front door, and Robbie listened to the thump of what sounded like the pizza box landing on their kitchen table and the creak of the old floorboards in the house.

Robbie had the TV on and was sitting cross legged on the sofa in the small living room. His dad had sawdust in his dark hair. He was lanky and tall, and Robbie took in his ring finger, on which he still wore his plain gold wedding band, even though Robbie's mom had been dead since he was five, from breast cancer. He didn't think his dad would ever take it off, as her loss had left a deep hole that would never heal.

He took in her big bright smile in the photo that was still on the wall. Young and beautiful. It left him empty.

"What were you up to today?" his dad said as he walked into the bathroom. Robbie could hear him taking a leak and then flushing.

"Oh, not much," he replied. He had just hung out with

his friends, but he couldn't shake the feeling that Brad thought he was so much better than him. Rodney Friessen owned a lot of land around them, but that was as far as it went. He had no say anywhere else. So why did it sting so much?

He listened to his dad wash his hands as he slipped off the sofa, hearing a pickup. He stopped at the open door and saw the big green truck, fairly new, parked beside his dad's older model Ford. He knew it was Rodney Friessen. Maybe that was why his heart was hammering in his chest so hard.

"Is someone there?" his dad called out, and Robbie had to force himself to swallow before he could answer.

"Mister Friessen," he said, then went to the table and sat down, taking in his empty bowl of cereal from that morning and the pizza box. He lifted the lid just as he heard the sharp rap on the door, and as he pulled out a piece, he took in the hardened expression on his dad's face.

His dad stood at the screen, staring out to what Robbie knew was Mr. Friessen staring back at him. It was another second, while he forced himself to take a bite of the tasteless pizza, before his dad opened the door.

"What do you want?" his dad said.

"I'm here to settle some things with you," Mr. Friessen said. There was nothing friendly in his voice, nothing friendly in his demand. For a minute, Robbie feared his dad would learn that he'd disobeyed him and had gone out to meet Brad and Neil and Jed. Then he'd basically be up shit creek, in trouble, grounded. For how long, he didn't have a clue. He tried to make himself small as he sat there in the chair, holding the pizza over his cereal bowl. His dad glanced once to him, and he took in the flash of anger that simmered there.

Rodney Friessen walked in and stood maybe five feet from him.

"I am so fucking tired of all your bullshit," Mr. Friessen said, "and you doing your damnedest to make my life a living hell. You've put up fences and blocked access to water for the cattle. You drive right across my field to the road when I asked you repeatedly to stay on the path by the crop of trees, the old logging road, yet you keep driving through where my cattle graze. You shoot your gun to scare them off. Then there's all the junk you leave every-where—old water tanks, scraps of metal. Look at this place! It looks like a fucking junkyard."

This was the norm, the fights with Mr. Friessen. Him and his dad would never be friends, which was likely why his dad didn't want him being friends with Neil, Brad, and Jed.

Yeah, his dad was mad, as well. He walked over to the fridge, pulled it open, and grabbed a bottle of beer, then used the side of the counter that was already chipped to take off the cap. Robbie heard it hit the floor. His dad took a big swallow and said nothing, but he didn't need to. Robbie knew when his dad was at the point of no return. There was that angry stage where he would yell, and that terrified him, and then there was the quiet, which was so much worse, because it meant that his dad had gone beyond anger. He remembered it well from after his mom had died, and he didn't want his dad there ever again.

"You took the fence down when you drove over the field," Mr. Friessen said. "The cows got out again."

"You think I want to drive down that old rutty road? No, that's ten minutes out of the way. I have every right to drive across the way I do. Those damn cows you have don't need to be here by my place. You have hundreds of acres and a lot of other land that's nowhere near us.

Hearing them at night, no! No more. Move them. You bet I fired off my rifle, and I'll keep doing it. I have a job I have to get to on time without dealing with a herd that blocks my way. I have bills to pay and don't have time to be sitting, waiting for cows to move."

Robbie forced himself to take another bite of pizza, wishing he could slip out and sneak off into his room with his dinner. He could put a pillow over his ears, and that would make it more bearable. But they would see him, considering Mr. Friessen was standing in his way, so he tried to shrink down so they wouldn't know he was there.

"Well, that's about to come to an end," Mr. Friessen said.

Robbie took in his dad and the way he held his beer as Mr. Friessen reached into his shirt pocket and pulled out a piece of paper.

"What's that?" his dad asked.

"Your eviction notice."

His dad actually started laughing. "You're crazy. I own this land, this place. You're a guest here, and I've heard about enough from you."

But Mr. Friessen held the paper out to him, and his dad finally took it and flipped it open. The expression on his face brought a sick feeling to Robbie's stomach. He clutched the pizza and couldn't take another bite, so he put it down in his bowl.

"You can't do this," his dad said. "This is impossible. You can't own this. This is my land, my house."

"Actually, not anymore. I warned you before what would happen to you if you kept aggravating me, if you kept being a problem."

His dad lowered his hand, still holding the paper, but the expression on his face reminded Robbie of how he'd been after his mom died. "This isn't legal. You can't just take my land. How?"

"I was going to put a lien on the lot, but my research revealed no official records on this place, just the fact that it was in your name and your dad's before that. Fixing that is easy enough when you know the right people. So hear me: You have twenty-four hours to clear out everything. This is now my land, my place. If you're still here when I come back this time tomorrow with the sheriff, with the law, who is on my side, I'll have you arrested for trespassing and whatever other charges we come up with. I guarantee you it will be enough that you'll never again see the light of day. Don't think I won't do it or can't do it."

All Robbie could do was stare at this man, who was his best friend's father, putting the screws to his dad. Then Mr. Friessen walked over to the door, and his gaze landed on Robbie for a second before it drifted back to his dad. There wasn't a smile or anything for him. He was looking at him with the same hatred he gave his dad.

"I mean it," he said. "Be gone, and take everything you want, because you will not be allowed back on this land or in this county, or I'll have you thrown in jail. Leave this town and don't come back, because if I see you anywhere near the county line, I'll follow through on my threat. I want you out of town tonight, and I don't want to see or hear from you again. I have plans for this place, and now, with you gone, this eyesore on my land will be gone too."

Then he was gone out the door, and his dad threw his beer bottle against the wall. It shattered, and Robbie jumped. His father roared, fisting his hands. It was a sound that terrified him and chilled him to the bone.

"Dad…" he cried out, scared as all hell.

His father just moved over to the wall in the kitchen and sank down to the floor, resting his arms on his knees and pressing his hands to his head. Robbie didn't know how long he sat there. He just stared at the pizza, his father, and the shattered glass on the floor.

"Okay, go pack your bags," his dad finally said to him.

"But where are we going to go? What are we going to do? Dad, this is our house, isn't it?"

It was suddenly real. His dad moved onto his knees and stood up, then started out of the room. He pressed his hand against the doorframe and didn't look back at Robbie. "Don't know," he said. "Just pack your bags. We got screwed, Robbie. That's what happens. Don't ever forget it. Rodney Friessen just stole everything from us, from you. He took your future. That man is the enemy. Don't ever forget it, Robbie. The Friessens are people you should hate. He's a bad man. These are bad people."

Chapter 5

It was getting late. Neil had left Brad at the treehouse after slipping away from home and leaving Jed. His dad was in the den, on the phone, and his mom was doing laundry in back.

Robbie should have been waiting for them at the treehouse, but he'd never come. They'd waited over an hour, he thought, the rain falling and the day a misty gray. He knew they wouldn't be able to wait much longer, so Brad had stayed and Neil had left.

He ran along the edge of the path to the open field, seeing Robbie's house in the distance. He expected to see smoke coming from the stovepipe, but there was nothing, and as he ran closer, he worried that Mr. Davis would be home, but he saw nothing as he walked around the front of the house to the open porch and up its four steps. All was quiet.

He knocked on the screen door. The inside door was closed, and he looked around but saw nothing, heard nothing.

Neil pulled open the screen door. The squeal should

have alerted anyone inside. He knocked again and listened. He expected to hear footsteps, anything, but there was nothing. He rested his hand on the doorknob, his heart thumping in his ears, and called out, "Robbie."

There was nothing, so he opened the door and stepped inside the kitchen. The fridge was open, and an empty bowl sat on the table.

"Robbie," he called out again as he stepped into the living room, seeing the walls were bare. The TV was gone, too, and there was nothing there but a sofa and a chair. All the photos were gone. Everything that made a house a home was no longer there. He went into the bathroom and saw it was empty, not a toothbrush or even a bar of soap. Then there was Robbie's room, with just the frame of a bed and a bare mattress. The closets were empty.

It took Neil a second to understand what he was looking at: an empty house, an empty home. His friend was just gone.

Neil was out of breath by the time he ran back to the treehouse.

"What took you so long? We have to go. Where's Robbie?" Brad called out as he climbed down.

"He's gone," Neil said. "The house is empty. There's nothing there. He's just gone. He didn't tell us he was leaving." Neil could feel the ache in his chest, and it was horrible, the loss.

Brad said nothing for a second and then started walking.

"Where are you going?" Neil called out.

"Home," Brad said. "We need to get home before Mom and Dad wonder where we are."

Neil had to run to catch up to him. "But what about Robbie?" he asked, still wondering how his friend could just leave without saying a word.

"Guess he's gone. What's there to say? Come on, Neil. We need to get home before we're in trouble." Brad hurried down the path that led back to the house.

"And that's it?" Neil said. He couldn't believe Brad could just shake it off like that. Robbie was his friend, his best friend. How could he just be gone?

"There's nothing to say, Neil. He left. They moved. There's nothing you can do about it. Gone is gone," Brad said.

All Neil could do as they walked side by side was look over to the east end of the property and wonder where his friend had gone.

Turn the page for a sneak peek of
STAY AWAY FROM MY DAUGHTER the next book in *THE FRIESSENS*
Available in print, eBook and audio

Stay Away From My Daughter

CIRCUMSTANCES THAT BROUGHT SARA & DEVON TOGETHER COULD ULTIMATELY TEAR THEM APART.

"When Sara's brutally attacked while leaving campus one night, Devon Reed comes to her rescue. But Devon's no white knight, and as all too often happens, no good deed goes unpunished. When Devon finds himself facing charges, it may only be Sara's faith in him that will save him this time."

CATLOU

Sara Friessen considers herself to be a typical teenager with an overprotective father, but when she is brutally attacked one night in a darkened parking lot she is saved by a mysterious handsome stranger who comes to her rescue. Only Devon Reed would never consider himself the kind of guy that could ever belong to her world, considering the ruthless dark world he belongs to and the fact he may know no more about the night she was attacked, and who really tried to hurt her.

Stay Away From My Daughter

CHAPTER 1

Her phone was ringing again, a ridiculous squawking rooster, a.k.a. the ringtone she'd assigned for her dad, and it echoed as she walked across the dimly lit parking lot of the college campus, which was half empty.

Sara Friessen was tempted once again not to answer.

She could do that. She had done that.

What would she pretend when her dad asked her why she hadn't answered her phone, which he paid for? Would she say she hadn't heard it, or would she tell the truth, which was that she was feeling as though she were on a tight leash and didn't want to have to face yet another inquisition?

Yeah, the latter definitely wouldn't go over well, considering how overprotective her dad was of his family. Scratch that—he was obsessively overprotective of his youngest daughter. His sons were a different story, a fact she'd pointed out to him was the pure definition of sexism. He'd told her to deal with it, because it was a man's role to protect his daughter, his wife, his family, and if that meant he was sexist, well, then he happily would take the title.

That was an argument she wasn't going to win with her dad.

She was pretty sure her dad had also put a tracking app on his phone so that he would know where she was every minute of the day. She wondered, truth be told, of the legality of that. It was a gray area of the law, considering she was his daughter, but her dad wouldn't take kindly to having that pointed out to him.

Her thumb hovered over the green and red buttons. Answer or decline? Andy Friessen was not a man she could keep blowing off, especially considering how late it was.

"I'm seriously on my way home," she answered and said, putting all the annoyance she could into her tone and letting out a frustrated sigh as she kept walking to her black pickup. Well, it was her dad's older model, which he'd insisted she drive, a fully loaded crew cab with leather seats —and yet another way to control what she was doing. He'd bought a newer version, also black. She'd have preferred to pick up a practical starter car for a few hundred bucks, something that would be entirely hers, not handed to her by her father. Just once, she'd like to be able to manage everything about her own life.

"Your father has called you twice, Sara," her mother said. "You were supposed to be home already. It's after ten."

She dug in her purse for the truck keys. It was looped over her shoulder with her laptop bag, and she could feel the tension that pulled across her shoulders as she felt the tightening of the leash around her neck. It was a joke between Sara and her mom, but at times like this, she swore she could feel the leather biting into her skin. It felt very real.

"Would it do any good to say I lost track of time? Seriously, Mom, I'm eighteen and would really appreciate it if you and Dad would ease up. Maybe you could remind him, since I'm pretty sure he's tracking me, that I'm capable of taking care of myself. I need some space. Stuff happens, and I'm going to get sidetracked when I'm studying. I thought you were going to talk to Dad about backing off. It's getting really fricking embarrassing when I'm studying with my friends and my phone keeps ringing, and there's Dad's name on my screen. Even my friends are starting to wonder about this incessant need to set a ridiculously early curfew and continually check in…"

"Are you done?" Her mom cut her off, and she could hear impatience and sternness, which she'd never heard in her mom's tone before. "Sara, you said you would be home at nine, and it's now eight after ten, to be exact. When you tell us you'll be home at a certain time and you don't show up, we worry, and then you don't answer your phone, so what are we to think?"

Something about the way her mom was talking let her know clearly that she'd gone too far and there was no talking her way out of this. She didn't have to be standing in front of Laura Friessen to realize how mad she really was.

"Where are you, exactly, right now?" Laura said. "Because you said you were going to meet friends to study and do homework at the coffeeshop. Let me remind you, Sara, if you lie to me, it will be the last thing you ever do, and even your father isn't going to step in and save you from such a fate. You go on and on about wanting to have freedom to date, to make your own decisions and be treated like an adult, but being eighteen means only that you're eighteen. You're still very much my daughter, and you're acting like a spoiled, inconsiderate brat. That makes you anything but a responsible adult, because responsible adults don't cause unneeded worry to their parents. This just confirms that you can't be trusted, and the short leash your father has you on is necessary, because you can't even pick up the damn phone and call us to say you're going to be late and tell us where you are. Then we wouldn't be sitting here, worrying and thinking you've been in an accident and are lying half dead on the side of the road!"

Holy shit! She'd never received this kind of scolding from her mom before, and she could feel the reprimand, realizing she should have picked up the phone instead of letting her friends goad her into not answering. The fact was that she'd been hanging out in the dorm party area on the comfy stained sofas, passing around a bottle of tequila, not doing homework in the coffeeshop. "Okay, I get it," she said, about to hang up. "I'm on my way home. Ten minutes and I'll be there."

"Twenty, Sara, because ten is what it takes if you're speeding, which is exactly what you're not going to do. And you didn't answer me about where you were. You said you were at the coffeeshop, but to our surprise, when we phoned the coffeeshop because we were thinking the worst, you want to know what they said?"

She pulled her phone away. "Fuck," she said under her breath. Of course she should have known. She and her friends had walked in and then right out of the empty coffeehouse. Tonight, everyone was hanging in the dorm, drinking, partying, and doing what every normal college kid did—nothing her parents should ever know about.

"I heard that, Sara," Laura said. "You want to tell me where you were, or do you need those twenty minutes to come up with a story? Let me remind you we already know the truth."

Oh, shit! Maybe her dad was having her followed. She

wouldn't put it past him, and she felt the hair on the back of her neck spike. It was a creepy feeling, and she found herself looking around the basically deserted lot, with just a few other cars. She could hear the faint noise of someone's music coming from the dorm she'd just left.

"It's not a big deal. We really did go into the coffeehouse but ended up in the dorm instead, where it was more comfortable on the sofas and less noisy." She winced, wondering if her nose grew, because the music blasting in the dorm had been anything but quiet. "Okay, Mom, I'm at the truck." She pressed the fob and heard the lock click. "Just unlocked it and am getting in, so I'll be home in twenty. You don't have to wait up…"

"We're waiting up, Sara," her mom said, and then the line went dead. Her mom had hung up on her.

She was seriously in deep shit. She stared at the phone, knowing her parents were likely going to give her an earful when she got home, and maybe it wasn't her dad she needed to be worried about. Would they be able to smell the two shots of tequila she'd had? She stopped at the truck after opening the door and held her hand up to her mouth, taking a whiff. Yeah, maybe some gum would help.

"Hey there, great party."

She glanced over her shoulder to the guy walking across the lot: light hair, blue jeans, and a green and white jersey.

"Sure," was all she said as she pulled open the back door of the truck and rested her computer bag on the seat. Then the guy was there in front of her as she tried to close the back door.

"So this is your truck? Fancy," he said with a smile. His wavy hair and face weren't familiar, but she could see the interest for her in his expression.

"Yeah, it is. Excuse me." She stepped back, but he

moved in front of her and was now standing between her and the open driver's door.

"So how about giving a guy a ride home? Maybe we can continue the party," he said.

She went to step around him, but he moved in front of her. He had about three, four inches on her in height and a solid build, too. She could smell the cigarette smoke on him.

"Sorry, not interested. My dad would kill me. I don't know you, and I'm kind of late, so no."

He didn't move, so she stepped back, taking in the darkened parking lot and wondering who this guy was.

"Well, that's not how it seemed in there." He gestured with his thumb to the dorm, which was still lit up, the party going strong. "I guess I'm confused. You were drinking with everyone, passing the bottle around, there for a good time. I noticed the looks." His hand was on her arm, his grip strong.

What the fuck? She pulled her arm away. "Hey, back off. I seriously think not. I was hanging with my friends, and if you think I was eyeing you up, you're delusional. I don't even remember seeing you. You're dreaming, buddy." She went to step around him again, but he took a step closer to her, right in her space, right in front of her. He was so quick, and she shrugged off his hand as it touched her shoulder again. He was so close she could smell the liquor, the lingering nicotine. That smell alone made her want to gag.

"I know you were interested." He leaned in, and it happened so fast, the hard kiss he pressed to her. She could taste the stink of beer, booze, a dirty ashtray, and she stepped back, pushed him hard with both her hands, pissed off.

"What the hell is your problem?" she snapped. "Stop…"

But he was in her face again so quick, and he grabbed her, his hand around her, pulling her against him. He was so damn strong, and she could feel the panic rising, the anger at the fact that he wouldn't back off.

"What the hell are you doing? Stop! Get your damn hands off me!" she yelled, and she fought against him as he held her tight.

He slapped his hand over her mouth. "Shut up," he hissed.

She fought like a wildcat, kicking, clawing, and she somehow managed to get his hand from her mouth and screamed, but he grabbed her hard and slammed her to the pavement.

It happened so fast. She could smell nicotine, his fingers pressed so hard over her mouth as she fought at the hand digging into her face, clawing with her fingers and kicking with the heels of her sneakers, using everything she had.

She bit on his hand hard, and he yelled. When he pulled his hand away, she screamed as loud as she could again, considering she was still struggling for breath. Then she felt the punch to her face and was slammed to the concrete again, hitting her jaw, scraping her cheek on the cement. The sting of the ground barely registered as she struggled with the weight of him on top of her. His hand was back around her mouth, and somehow he'd pinned one of her arms behind her back, the weight of his body pulling so hard that she thought he'd wrench her arm from its socket.

She couldn't pull her arm out, and he was working the button of her jeans, the zipper. She could feel the tug as he pushed her into the concrete, and she could hear him fumbling with his own belt, feeling his weight grinding her into the ground. She fought and squirmed and struggled to breathe, because now he was choking her, his hand squeezing her throat.

This couldn't be happening, but he was strong—brutally strong. He overpowered her, and his large hand squeezed so hard she couldn't breathe, knowing that she was going to pass out. She couldn't get air, and he was going to rape her, hurt her, maybe kill her. She was getting weaker, struggling for a breath and then another. She couldn't pass out, not like this, but even though she fought, she couldn't get his hand off her throat.

It couldn't end like this. This wasn't fair. She just needed a breath, but she couldn't move.

She vaguely heard someone yell, and then suddenly all the weight on her was gone. His hand was gone.

She gasped, dragging in a breath, her throat aching. She was gasping on her hands and knees, coughing and fighting to fill her lungs as she crawled to the side of the truck. Her jeans were undone.

She heard a man yell again, then the impact of a fist, a scuffle, fighting. Someone was slammed against the truck. She felt the rumble. She lifted her hand to her throat, and then she struggled to get up. The two men barely registered, one hitting the other. She was on her knees again, gasping.

The truck door was still open, and a guy was punching her assailant over and over. Then somehow he was gone, running, and the other one started after him but turned back and took her in. A fear she'd never felt before had paralyzed her. Somehow, her hands shaking, she righted her jeans and buttoned them up.

Then her rescuer was there in front of her, and she felt gravel digging into the palms of her hands as she tried to push herself up. He had a strong jaw and shaved dark hair, deep brown eyes, and two diamond studs in his ears.

"You okay?" he said. His voice was deep, and he watched her, waiting for her to answer, but she couldn't get her brain to register. She knew he was the one who had saved her, but she couldn't get her tongue to move. She clutched at her throat, which still ached.

He didn't come any closer, and she instinctively backed away, scooting on her butt, feeling the hard wall of a tire at her back. She couldn't move any farther. What was wrong with her?

He didn't touch her or move closer, as he was now squatting down, holding his large hand out, and she just stared at it. There was no way in hell she could touch him.

"You're hurt," he said. "Your face. I'm going to call the police right now. Did you know him?" He had a cell phone out and was now standing, and he moved back, giving her space.

She couldn't move as she took him in. He was talking to someone now, but what he was saying didn't register. She still couldn't get her head around the fact that she'd just been attacked, how fast it had happened. She was feeling catatonic. It was dark except for the lights in the parking lot, and then she heard the siren.

He was there again, squatting down in front of her, but she just sat, frozen, staring at her purse, which was lying on the ground—her keys too, and her wallet. "Can I help you up?" he said. "The police and help are on the way." He still didn't move closer.

What could she say? She took in her purse and then crawled on her knees over to it to stuff everything back inside. He didn't touch her, and now she took in his face, the hint of mocha to his skin. She just shook her head, as she couldn't get her tongue to move. Why was she so stuck on his large hands?

"You're hurt, your face, your neck." He gestured toward her.

"I'm fine, it's okay. Who was he?" she said. Her voice sounded so odd, and she was shaking—not just shaking, trembling. It had started inside her and moved outside. He didn't try to touch her, but he didn't pull his gaze from her. She should feel safe, but she was worried about the other guy. What if he came back?

"You're not fine, and it wasn't okay," he said. "Don't be so polite. He assaulted you. I don't know him, sorry. I was going to go after him, but I wasn't sure how badly you were hurt. So you didn't know him?"

She pressed her hand to the side of the truck and went on her knees again. She could see her hand shaking. The back of it was scraped, and beads of blood welled as she stood up. He did too as if getting ready to catch her, the way he watched her. He was damn tall, wearing a red and white jacket and what looked like a gold class ring on his finger. Just then, the sheriff's car pulled up.

"I should go home," she said. "I'm late. I was supposed to be home already. My dad, my parents…they're going to be so mad at me. I said I was on my way home…" She stopped talking because she couldn't make sense of what she was saying.

He glanced only once to the cop car and back to her, shoving his hands in his pockets. "Look, I can tell how shaken up you are. Some guy messed with you. You're not okay. The police are here. You need to talk to them so they can catch that guy. You should go to the hospital too, get checked out. And you shouldn't be driving now."

The lights of the cop car were still flashing, and she

was stuck on how kind his eyes were. He was tall, solid. She didn't remember ever seeing him before.

A deputy climbed out of the cruiser, wearing a tan uniform, and he walked over to her, glancing sternly at the man who'd saved her. She didn't know what to say. Her throat ached, her face hurt, and she just wanted to get in the truck and drive away. She couldn't make sense of what had just happened.

She just shook her head as she held her keys and clutched her purse against her chest, then touched the door of her open truck. She was in a fog and just going through the motions.

"Whoa, whoa, hang on a second, here," said the deputy, who grabbed the open truck door. "You can't go anywhere. I need you to tell me what happened here. A call came in about an assault…"

She took him in. He had light hair, and she wondered for a minute if he'd touch her. She had to step back, shifting her glance to the other guy. The way he took in the cop, she wasn't sure what to make of it.

"She was attacked," the guy said. "He was trying to rape her. I heard her scream, and I pulled the guy off. We fought, but he got away. He took off between the buildings." This stranger who had saved her didn't pull his gaze from her.

The cop was now saying something into a walkie-talkie attached to his shirt. "There's an ambulance on the way. How about we start with your names? Did either of you know the assailant?"

"My name's Sara, Sara Friessen. I did nothing wrong. I just want to go home. I don't know him, even though he said I was flirting with him. I don't remember seeing him. He said he was in the dorm, at the party. I just don't recall. There were so many people there. I don't know everyone. I have to go. I was supposed to be home already. My parents are waiting," she said, feeling the emotion squeeze her chest. Although she'd lied before to her mom and dad, she realized that as angry as they had been, now they were going to be furious. She'd really screwed up this time.

"Okay, Sara, let's call your parents," the deputy said. "And then I need to ask you if you've been drinking."

"Lorhainne Eckhart is one of my go to authors when I want a guaranteed good book. So many twists and turns, but also so much love and such a strong sense of family."

(LORA W., REVIEWER)

New York Times & USA Today bestseller Lorhainne Eckhart is best known for writing Raw Relatable Real Romance where "Morals and family are running themes." As one fan calls her, she is the "Queen of the family saga." (aherman) writing "the ups and downs of what goes on within a family but also with some suspense, angst and of course a bit of romance thrown in for good measure."

Follow Lorhainne on Bookbub to receive alerts on New Releases and Sales and join her mailing list at Lorhainne-Eckhart.com for her Monday Blog, all book news, give-aways and FREE reads. With over 120 books, audiobooks, and multiple series published and available at all, retailers now translated into six languages. She is a multiple recipient of the Readers' Favorite Award for Suspense and Romance, and lives in the Pacific Northwest on an island, is the mother of three, her oldest has autism and she is an advocate for never giving up on your dreams.

"Lorhainne Eckhart has this uncanny way of just hitting the spot every time with her books."

(CAROLINE L., REVIEWER)

The O'Connells: *The O'Connells of Livingston, Montana are not your typical family. A riveting collection of stories surrounding the ups and downs of what goes on within a family but also with some suspense, angst and of course a bit of romance thrown in for good measure. "I thought I loved the Friessens, but I absolutely adore the O'Con-nell's. Each and every book has different genres of stories, but the one thing in common is how she is able to wrap it around the family, which is the heart of each story." (C. Logue)*

The Friessens: *An emotional big family romance series, the Friessen family siblings find their relationships tested, lay their hearts on the line, and discover lasting love! "Lorhainne Eckhart is one of my go to authors when I want* *a guaranteed good book. So many twists and turns, but also so much love and such a strong sense of family." (Lora W., Reviewer)*

The Parker Sisters: *The Parker Sisters are a close-knit family, and like any other family they have their ups and downs. Eckhart has crafted another intense family drama… "The character development is outstanding, and the emotional investment is high…" (Aherman, Reviewer)*

The McCabe Brothers: *Join the five McCabe siblings on their journeys to the dark and dangerous side of love! An intense, exhilarating collection of romantic thrillers you won't want to miss. — "Eckhart has a new series that is definitely worth the read. The queen of the family saga started this series with a spin-off of her wildly successful Friessen series." From a Readers' Favorite award—winning author and "queen of the family saga" (Aherman)*

Billy Jo McCabe Mystery: *The social worker and the cop, an unlikely couple drawn together on a small, secluded Pacific Northwest island where nothing is as it seems. Protecting the innocent comes at a cost, and what seems to be a sleepy, quiet town is anything but.*

Lorhainne loves to hear from her readers! You can connect with me at:
www.LorhainneEckhart.com
lorhainneeckhart.le@gmail.com

Also by Lorhainne Eckhart

The Outsider Series
The Forgotten Child (Brad and Emily)
A Baby and a Wedding *(An Outsider Series Short)*
Fallen Hero (Andy, Jed, and Diana)
The Awakening (Andy and Laura)
Secrets (Jed and Diana)
Runaway (Andy and Laura)
Overdue *(An Outsider Series Short)*
The Unexpected Storm (Neil and Candy)
The Wedding (Neil and Candy)

The Friessens: A New Beginning
The Deadline (Andy and Laura)
The Price to Love (Neil and Candy)
A Different Kind of Love (Brad and Emily)
A Vow of Love, A Friessen Family Christmas

The Friessens
The Reunion
The Bloodline (Andy & Laura)
The Promise (Diana & Jed)
The Business Plan (Neil & Candy)
The Decision (Brad & Emily)
First Love (Katy)
Family First
Leave the Light On
In the Moment
In the Family
In the Silence

In the Charm
Unexpected Consequences
It Was Always You
The First Time I Saw You
Welcome to My Arms
Welcome to Boston
I'll Always Love You
Ground Rules
A Reason to Breathe
You Are My Everything
Anything For You
The Homecoming
Stay Away From My Daughter
The Bad Boy
A Place of Our Own
The Visitor
All About Devon
Long Past Dawn
How to Heal a Heart
Keep Me In Your Heart

The O'Connells
The Neighbor
The Third Call
The Secret Husband
The Quiet Day
The Commitment
The Missing Father
The Hometown Hero
Justice
The Family Secret
The Fallen O'Connell
The Return of the O'Connells
And The She Was Gone

The Stalker
The O'Connell Family Christmas
The Girl Next Door
Broken Promises
The Gatekeeper
The Hunted

The McCabe Brothers
Don't Stop Me (Vic)
Don't Catch Me (Chase)
Don't Run From Me (Aaron)
Don't Hide From Me (Luc)
Don't Leave Me (Claudia)
Out of Time

A Billy Jo McCabe Mystery
Nothing As it Seems
Hiding in Plain Sight
The Cold Case
The Trap
Above the Law
The Stranger at the Door
The Children
The Last Stand
The Charity
The Sacrifice

The Street Fighter
Finding Home
Finding Honor

The Wilde Brothers
The One (Joe and Margaret)
The Honeymoon, A Wilde Brothers Short

Friendly Fire (Logan and Julia)
Not Quite Married, A Wilde Brothers Short
A Matter of Trust (Ben and Carrie)
The Reckoning, A Wilde Brothers Christmas
Traded (Jake)
Unforgiven (Samuel)
The Holiday Bride

Married in Montana

His Promise
Love's Promise
A Promise of Forever

The Parker Sisters

Thrill of the Chase
The Dating Game
Play Hard to Get
What We Can't Have
Go Your Own Way
A June Wedding

Kate & Walker

One Night
Edge of Night
Last Night

Walk the Right Road Series

The Choice
Lost and Found
Merkaba
Bounty
Blown Away: The Final Chapter
He Came Back

The Saved Series
Saved
Vanished
Captured

Single Titles
Loving Christine

www.ingramcontent.com/pod-product-compliance
Lightning Source LLC
Chambersburg PA
CBHW021128070726
47591CB00014B/1700